STORM THE NIGHT

THE ENFORCERS

JANE HINCHEY

BAYWOLF PRESS

AUTHOR'S NOTE

Welcome to "The Enforcers" series—a collection that has truly been on a remarkable journey. When I first embarked on this adventure, I could hardly have imagined the twists and turns it would take. Initially self-published under my own name, these stories found a new identity with the pen name Zahra Stone, and even underwent a title transformation along the way. Now, they've come full circle, returning to their original author.

While I'm predominantly known for my cozy mysteries, "The Enforcers" holds a special place in my heart. It's a series that has evolved with me and witnessed the various stages of my writing career. I'm thrilled to present these stories to you once more, enriched by their journey and under my own name again.

To stay updated with all my literary escapades, including the latest on "The Enforcers" and my cozy mysteries, I warmly invite you to sign up for my newsletter. It's the best way to keep in the loop about new releases and exclusive content.

You can sign up for my newsletter here:

Janehinchey.com/subscribe

Thank you for joining me on this incredible journey. I hope you enjoy the world of "The Enforcers" as much as I have enjoyed bringing it to you.

xoxo

Jane

ABOUT THIS BOOK

I'm Paige Shelton, and my life in Maxxan, Texas, is anything but ordinary. By day, I'm a graphic designer with a designer wardrobe. By night? I'm an unlikely vampire slayer in killer stilettos, hunting the bloodsuckers that lurk in my town. Everything changes when I meet Nate Wilder, a vampire who's as dangerous as he is alluring.

Nate offers me a deal I can't ignore: help him hunt a rogue ghoul, and I earn my freedom. Working with him, I start questioning everything I've been taught about vampires. With my family and friends in danger, trust becomes a luxury I can barely afford.

As Nate and I delve deeper into the shadows of Maxxan, our bond intensifies. Caught in a web of secrets and lies, I'm torn between my duty as a slayer and the forbidden allure of my vampire ally. With each revelation, the line between friend and foe blurs. Can I trust Nate as we stand against an ancient evil, or will my heart lead me into peril? 'Storm the Night' is a tale of passion, mystery, and the courage to find truth in the darkness.

Author's Note: The saga continues with Storm the Night, first known to readers as Blood & Fire, part of the SIA series by Jane Hinchey. It briefly donned the guise of Zahra Stone's Storm the Night, but now it reclaims its original identity, albeit with a few touch-ups. This edition, while not extensively edited, has been refined and is re-emerging under my true name. Dive back into this enchanting world, where the story's heart remains the same, but its beat resounds more clearly than ever.

"Do you really think you can hold me?" The vampire pulled at the burning ropes restraining him, his eyes as black as night as he challenged me.

"Sure do," I replied. My lasso of flame had done an excellent job so far, provided you could tolerate the stench of burning flesh. It had taken me quite some time to hone my skills and manage the lasso, and pull forth my other fire demon skills at the same time. But practice makes perfect, and here we were.

Already the fire was having its desired effect—the vampire's fangs appeared as he winced with each flex of his wrist. The flame wouldn't kill him, but it hurt like the devil and would slow him down. I'd learned that from my cousin Rae.

"Who do you work for?" I asked.

He grinned, his fangs glinting, then stretched as if to prove that my burning restraints didn't faze him, that he'd be free soon enough, and when that happened, he promised retribution.

"No one."

"Liar," I called forth my fire—a sword of flame. To be honest, it wasn't really a sword; it was any pointy object I needed to conjure for my needs at any particular time. Sometimes it was a spear. Sometimes a dagger. Sometimes an arrow. But I liked the sword the best.

With deft movements, I cut away his shirt, exposing the pale flesh of his chest. Although his skin may have been a pale white color I didn't find appealing, the muscles beneath rippled, and I had to admit—this guy had abs to die for. I swallowed, refusing to be distracted.

As if he knew, he grinned. "Like what you see?"

I ignored him, tracing the tip of the sword down his chest, leaving a dark burn that sizzled and popped before it healed. This was why it was so much fun. I could exact hours of torture on him, and he'd continue to recover—just as his wrists were doing from my lasso. Burn to the bone. Heal. Over and over again.

He glanced at his chest. "Is that supposed to frighten me?"

I considered the question. "Well, I've been taking out vampires for a while now. I've got a blade to your heart, so yes, you should be afraid." His expression was still amused. Why did they think that just because I was a petite female, they shouldn't be afraid? They misjudged me over and over.

My phone began vibrating, and I put away my sword to pull my cell from the pocket of my swirling Stella McCartney summer dress. Yes, a dress with pockets - a rare find, which was why I bought the same dress in three different patterns. Today's was my favorite, white with red cherries. My red-heeled Louboutin's matched perfectly. Swiping the screen, I put the phone to my ear, not taking my eyes from the vampire pinned in front of me.

"Yeah?" I answered.

"Paige, where are you? You said you'd pick up the cake." Mom's voice came through loud and clear, and I cursed.

"Sorry, Mom. Lost track of time. I've got the cake. I'll be there soon."

"Well. Hurry."

"On my way," I lied. I'd yet to extract

information on the Gunslinger from any of the vampires that I'd caught, interrogated, and killed in the last two months. The body count was mounting, and I was no closer than when I started.

Rae and her boyfriend, SIA Agent Jordan Buchanan, were in Redmeadows, where Rae was training to become a bona fide agent herself. In the meantime, Maxxan was vulnerable—I didn't care what Jordan had to say about it. Just because the Red Witch had removed the spell that allowed vampires to walk in daylight, it didn't eradicate our current vampire problem—it just moved it to a nocturnal time slot.

Plus, there was something else, something one of the vampires had hinted at that had piqued my interest. There was something else in Maxxan, and trouble was brewing. Sadly, I hadn't been able to get any more information from that vampire before he expired.

"Got a date?" the vampire in front of me drawled with feigned interest. He should have been afraid, and it made me mad that he wasn't. They all underestimated me, thinking I was just a pretty little girl playing around. *I'm a vampire slayer, dammit. You should be quaking in terror.*

"Actually, I do," I replied, sliding the phone back

into my pocket. "So I've got to wrap this up, I'm afraid."

"What a shame."

"It is. I was hoping to spend more time with you," I agreed, calling forth my flame once more.

"Maybe another day?" He quirked an eyebrow. I always admired that trait in a male, but now wasn't the time to be admiring what he could do with his various body parts.

"That won't be possible—I'm afraid you won't be available." Then I slid the flaming sword into his heart.

His face registered surprise, his eyes widening as his body slowly disintegrated into ash at my feet. Pulling my fire back to myself, I stepped back, cursing that I'd gotten his ash on my shoes. Walking over to the card table, I dug through my oversized Kate Spade handbag for a tissue and wiped the gray dust from my Louboutin's, made sure my dress was clean, tightened the ponytail that held my hair high on the top of my head, then slung my bag over my shoulder. I had a birthday party to get to.

Locking the warehouse behind me, I walked to my car, glancing around to make sure I hadn't been seen. The warehouse had been a great find—its current owner had no use for it and had been more than happy to allow me to use it for free. Of course, he didn't know what I was using it for. He thought I was an artist—which I am, of sorts. My art is torture, and my canvas is a vampire's flesh.

Sliding behind the wheel, I tilted the rearview mirror to check my makeup. Winged eyeliner was still in place, long dark lashes looked phenomenal, blue eyes were bright, and freckles were covered with immaculately applied foundation. I pulled out my lipstick, touched up my red lips, made a kissing motion at myself, and then pulled out, heading to my apartment.

Tonight's hunting expedition had been unexpected. It was early, only just gone seven, and I wasn't in my usual hunting ground—the nightclub Enchant. I'd been in the store buying wine for tonight. When the vamp had approached me, I'd taken a chance since I hadn't intended to hunt tonight at all. It was Dad's birthday, and I had a family dinner to get to. But the opportunity was too good to resist.

Letting the vampire think he'd lured me in, I suggested we use my car. Stupid fool thinking he could seduce me, drink my blood, that I was an unsuspecting human. Instead, I got him in my car, restrained him with my lasso, and the rest, as they say, is history. I'd learned early on that I made excellent vampire bait, that they were attracted to my pretty, feminine features, my designer clothes, my tiny size, and my delicate appearance. I sniggered at their misconceptions.

It was a quick ten-minute drive to my apartment above the bakery on the main strip of Maxxan. As a freelance graphic designer, I had a limited budget. Considering I spent more on clothes and shoes than I should, the tiny apartment that always smelled like baked goods was all I could afford. Not that I'm complaining, I love it. It's cozy and suits my needs perfectly.

Running upstairs, I retrieved the birthday cake from the fridge, then headed out to Mom and Dad's. It was the first big family get-together since Uncle Frank had been arrested—we'd all been shocked when it was revealed he was working with the vampires to produce the mind-altering drug Rampage. Jordan had stopped him, and he was currently incarcerated at SIA in Redmeadows.

Poor Rae. It must have been a further blow for her to discover her own dad had orchestrated for her to be committed to a mental asylum just to get her out of the way. My cousin and I had been close growing up, but when she was sent away at eighteen, we'd lost touch. When she'd been released from the Institute, she'd headed to Alaska and had been gone from Maxxan for years—she'd only returned for Grandma's funeral, and that was when everything had gone pear-shaped. But the silver lining was Rae had found love—with Jordan. I was happy for her and only a little envious. I'd had a string of boyfriends, but nothing serious. No one I'd be prepared to settle down for a happily ever after with.

"Finally!" My brother, Cody, opened the car door before I had a chance to turn off the engine.

"Geez, what's the rush?" Lifting the cake box from the passenger seat, I handed it to him. "Take this."

"Mom's in a panic. She wants everything to be perfect."

"Pft. Our family doesn't do perfect." I snorted, grabbed my bag from the floor, and felt around for the bottle of wine I'd purchased earlier.

"Paige." His warning hurt. I'd been nothing but supportive of my family. Always. How dare he suggest otherwise?

"Cody," I responded, shooting him an angry glare.

He grinned and then apologized. "Sorry—Mom's rubbing off on me. I feel as wired as she is."

"It'll be fine. Stop worrying." I followed him inside, where Mom was busy in the kitchen.

"Oh, good, you're here. Did you get the cake?" She whirled past, dropping a kiss on my cheek as she lifted plates down from a cupboard.

"Yes, I brought the cake." I tilted my head to indicate to Cody to put it in the fridge. He did.

"What's up, Mom?" Sliding my arm around her waist, I forced her to stop her frenzied rushing around. She sucked in a deep breath and blew it out, then laughed. "You know, I don't really know?"

"Tonight will be fine. It'll all be fine."

"It's just... Deb. She's really isolated herself since Frank was arrested. I've barely seen her, even though I've reached out a dozen times. I thought we were close, best friends, but..."

"She probably just needs some time, Mom. It was pretty epic, what happened with Uncle Frank. I mean, could you imagine if it were Dad?"

"I'd be so hurt!" Mom cried, her hand pressing on her cheek. "And embarrassed."

"Maybe Aunt Deb is feeling some of that, hmmm? We just need to continue to be her family—

continue to be her friends," I suggested, squeezing her waist.

Mom smiled, patting my arm. "You have a wise head on your shoulders, Paige. I always said you were an old soul."

"Right. What can I do to help?" Releasing her, I indicated the kitchen bench where dishes of food were in various stages of preparation.

"Here. Take this through." She handed me a platter of dip, biscuits, and carrot sticks. "To snack on until dinner is ready."

I headed into the dining room with the platter. It was the first time the family had been together since the shit hit the fan, and I had questions that demanded answers. Tonight was the night.

Dinner had been a bust. I learned nothing new. Mom had vetoed any conversation regarding vampires, Rampage, fire demons, pretty much any topic of interest. Aunt Deb had turned up looking pale and fragile—her appearance was enough to keep my mouth shut. She looked like she'd shatter into a million pieces at any moment, and my heart hurt for her. I'd seen that look before on my older sister Katie. I hoped to never see it again.

But today was a new day. Standing in front of my corkboard, I studied the pieces of paper pinned there—my research. I stared blindly at the names I'd compiled, waiting for a clue, a connection, to leap out at me. I got nothing.

Sighing, I finished my toast and wiped my hands absently on the legs of my red Capri pants. Even though I worked for myself from home, I still maintained dress standards—no slouching around in yoga gear or PJs for this girl. Today I was in Ralph Lauren's white midriff lace top and the red capris. On my feet were Saint Laurent sandals. Makeup was minimal: black wingtip eyeliner, mascara, and a slick of gloss on my lips. I'd re-apply when I went out hunting tonight.

Turning my back on the corkboard, I sat at the small desk tucked in the corner of my living room and turned on my computer. I had a book cover to finish for an author, a flyer to design for a local florist, and a new startup that wanted a logo and business card design. Even with the work I brought in via my business, I could only snap up my designer threads when they were on sale—thank God for online shopping!

With music pumping, I set to work, and the hours flew. The sun was dipping below the horizon, bathing my apartment in orange hues just as I hit send on my final email for the day. Stretching out my cramping muscles, I stood, turning off my computer and thinking about what to have for dinner. Unlike Katie, who was a whizz in the kitchen, I had zero culinary skills. If it wasn't takeout, it was a frozen dinner. My face lit up when I remembered Mom had sent me home with a plate of leftovers—win!

While the leftovers were reheating in the microwave, I ran a bath—a long hot soak at the end of a day spent in front of a monitor was in order. Then it would be time to hunt. Just the thought of it had my lips curling in anticipation—I couldn't say *why* I enjoyed it. Maybe because it was my forbidden secret, the taboo. And also, my over-inquisitive nature. I needed to find answers, and I was prepared to employ any means necessary to get them. Cody often referred to me as bloodthirsty—I'd see something, I'd want it, I'd make sure I got it. No matter what it took, no matter who I had to walk over to get it. If only he knew!

ENCHANT WAS RELATIVELY quiet when I arrived, but I'd expected it. Had planned on it, which was why I came early, to scope out the best spot to lay in wait for any vampires who thought I'd make a tasty snack. I was confident tonight wouldn't take long before I got a bite. In black leather pants, five-inch Jimmy Choo stilettos, and a leather bustier with a zip-up front covered by six buckles, I was dark, sexy, and irresistible. I'd pulled my hair up into a messy knot on top of my head, leaving a few tendrils loose. My makeup was dark, with sultry eyes, extra heavy on the eyeliner. Lips full and painted blood red.

Ordering a vodka and cranberry, I settled in to wait. Three drinks later, I was frowning. The nightclub had filled up; the music was pumping; in fact, it was a little too loud, and I was starting to get a headache. Numerous men had attempted to pick me up, but none of them were what I wanted. A vampire. But so far, I hadn't sensed any, which was highly unusual for Enchant.

When I'd first started hunting, I hadn't been able to identify the vampires from the humans; it wasn't until I'd get them alone that they revealed themselves. Vampires went for my neck; humans went for my boobs. Now I'd gotten good at reading their energy. Instead of wasting time on a drunk human who wanted to get into my pants, I could focus on my real prey. The bloodsuckers invading my town.

It was getting late, and I was tired. Waiting at the bar, I promised myself one more drink, and then I'd call it quits. I'd just raised the glass to my lips when I felt it. A change in the air. I slowly swiveled, scoping out the nightclub, trying to find him. For it had to be a vampire. I assumed it was a male purely because all the vampires I'd captured so far had been male.

Then my eyes locked onto the most sinfully delicious man I'd ever seen. Tall, over six-foot, with broad shoulders and dark hair—from here, it looked black, but that could be attributed to the club's dim lighting. Dressed in black jeans and a close-fitting long-sleeve black T-shirt that molded to his chiseled body. He looked dark, dangerous, and undeniably sexy. Raising my glass to my lips, I took a long, slow sip, unable to tear my eyes away.

When he looked up and spotted me staring at him, I knew. For despite his stunning gray eyes, whisker-stubbled jaw, and sensual mouth—he was a vampire. *Bingo*. We continued to stare at each other for several drawn-out seconds, his gaze intent, mine seductive—I hoped. When he bent to talk to the woman by his side, I quickly gulped my drink to calm my suddenly racing heart. Then he was walking toward me, his gait smooth and powerful, as he weaved his way through the crowd to my side.

"Hello, handsome," I said in my most alluring voice.

"Hey," he responded, his voice as smooth as honey. I looked into his gray eyes, mesmerized. "Can I buy you a drink?" he asked.

"Sure." I smiled. He signaled the bartender, and faster than I could blink, a fresh drink appeared in front of me. If only I could garner that type of service.

"Are you here by yourself?" He asked, leaning one elbow on the bar, his body angled toward me.

"Do you want me to be?" With him, my flirting felt stilted, unnatural. With the others, it had been an easy act—flutter my lashes, act coy, and they were all mine. But with him? With him, it was different. I didn't feel in control at all. Along with his blinding good looks came a sense of power, one that sent me reeling.

"I'd like it if you were." His voice was low and intimate, and I shivered. I opened my mouth to reply, but words failed me. His smile deepened, and his eyes moved from my mouth to my neck, which I stretched reflexively. He traced a finger along my jaw, and I shivered, thrown off guard.

"Shall we go?" He asked. I felt dazed and slightly panicked. Was I in over my head with this vampire? No, I scolded myself. You've got this. You're a kick-ass vampire hunter. Pull yourself together. Just because he looks like he could ride you every which way, including Sunday, does not mean he gets a free pass.

"Go?" I tore my gaze from him and watched the dance floor instead, trying to focus on anything but him. I needed to get my head straight.

"Mmmm." His fingers wrapped around a loose tendril of my hair and toyed with it. "Somewhere quieter. I'd like to... get to know you better."

Nice. Usually, I was the one trying to lure my prey out of the bar. They were always eager, blindly agreeing to get in the car with me since I knew a place where we wouldn't be disturbed. Of course, they'd been expecting my apartment, and even when they'd stepped over the threshold into the warehouse, they hadn't twigged, hadn't realized I didn't need to invite them in. I assumed they were in the early stages of bloodlust and blindly followed, intent on nothing but sinking their fangs into my vein. Then I'd bring out my fire lasso, and well, we all know how that ends.

"That sounds good," I responded, a little surprised by just how excited my voice was.

He chuckled, brushing my neck with the back of his fingers. I shivered. I wasn't sure if it was from fear or pleasure—how could I possibly be attracted to a vampire? They were the enemy. I needed to hurry this along, get this over with, and remove the temptation standing so close to me.

"What's your name?" I asked, easing away from him, giving myself some breathing room that I so desperately needed. For a moment, I'd forgotten where I was and what I was doing here.

"Does it matter?" he murmured.

"I guess not." He was right. It didn't matter at all.

"Let's go." Placing my drink on the bar, I led the way outside, feeling him close behind me. He was so damn tall. He towered over me and made me feel even smaller than I was. At five feet two and one hundred and three pounds, I was, as someone had once described, a pocket rocket. I used it to my advantage because vampires, hell, men in general, thought I was weak. Easily subdued. Their assumptions were seriously misplaced, for even without my fire demon abilities, I knew how to defend myself. I'd been studying Gilan Cae martial arts since I was twelve, and I was damn good at it.

"My car's this way." He touched my elbow, guiding me toward a dark SUV.

"Oh, I thought we'd take mine." I pointed to my blue Volkswagen Golf parked not ten feet away. I'd need my car to get back home—and I didn't want to have to deal with his vehicle being abandoned outside the warehouse.

He stopped and looked down at me for a moment—I couldn't see his face clearly in the dark, but he appeared to be thinking about it before shrugging and heading toward my car.

I was nervous. I didn't usually get nervous, not anymore; I had my act down pat. Flirt with them, make them think they were in control, that they were going to get what they wanted. It was easy, and I was confident. But with him, I wasn't so sure, and that made me nervous. My heart rate was up, and I could feel sweat beading on my upper lip.

In the small confines of the car, his presence was even more overwhelming.

"Are you wearing cologne?" I asked, fastening my seatbelt and sliding the key in the ignition.

"No," he replied, buckling his belt. Oh. That meant this effect was all him. *Damn.* I pulled out from the curb, and an uneasy silence descended. Usually, they were chatty, telling me how sexy I was, how much they wanted me, all of that stuff they thought I wanted to hear. Not this guy. I glanced at him out of the corner of my eye. He appeared relaxed, his hands resting loosely on his knees. He was looking straight ahead, not paying me the slightest bit of attention.

Thankfully, the drive to the warehouse was short, and my nerves were starting to change to anticipation. I rolled to a stop and killed the engine, releasing my belt. It was dark here. I'd intentionally broken the street lamp outside and removed the bulb from above the warehouse door—no need to draw attention to what went on inside.

Before I could get out of the car, he turned to face me, grabbing my hand.

"You're sure you want to do this?" he asked, his face unreadable. Again, this was something that had never happened before. Usually, they were helping me out of the car at this point, all handsy, brushing my hair from my neck and practically drooling at the prospect of my blood. Again, not this guy.

"I'm sure." I smiled, showing my even white teeth. I'd perfected this smile. It was the one that looked like I was happy, but if you looked carefully, if you looked hard enough, you'd know it didn't reach my eyes. I was acting. But they never looked hard enough.

He studied me for a moment longer before releasing my hand and opening his door. *Right, we're doing this.* It was vital that he walk into the warehouse ahead of me. It gave me the element of surprise and allowed me the few scant seconds I needed to call forth my flame and trap him.

"After you." He stood just in front of the door, gesturing me to go ahead of him. *Shit!*

"You go. I'm right behind you." I returned his gesture, trying to usher him ahead of me.

"I insist, ladies first." He stood resolute, and I cursed his good manners. I had no choice but to enter ahead of him; otherwise, we'd both be standing outside arguing over who went first, and that would look not only foolish but suspicious, and I needed to keep him oblivious as to what was about to happen.

"Fine." I'd muttered it under my breath, but I caught the smirk that curled his lip as I stepped forward. He'd heard me, not surprising given his vampire-enhanced hearing. I didn't want to alert him to my fire demon status, so rather than lighting the warehouse with a fireball, I flicked the light switch. A single bulb illuminated a small area, but it was all the light I needed.

"Nice place," he drawled. When I turned to face him, I was not expecting what happened next. He punched me in the side of the head. Hard. So hard I was out, crumpling to the floor in an unconscious heap.

THREE

"Urgh." I groaned, my head throbbing. "Whaa?"

"Finally." The sound of his voice had my eyes springing open. *What the hell?* Confused, I tried to get my head around my current situation… which was chained to a pole in my very own warehouse. My arms were stretched above my head, my toes barely reached the floor, and my head hurt like a son of a bitch.

I immediately summoned my flame and tried to burn the chains keeping me captive, but all I managed to do was heat the chain until it burned my skin. *Damn it.* Then I tried my lasso, but with my hands restrained, I couldn't wield it, and it flopped around in front of me, useless.

"Finished?" He was sitting on the fold-out chair I'd bought for this very purpose. Interrogating my captives. Only this time, I was on the receiving end, and I had a feeling I wasn't going to like what was to come.

"What's going on?" I demanded, tugging at my aching wrists.

"You tell me." I didn't like being on the receiving end, I decided. Not at all. Tugging harder, I twisted and turned, trying to dislodge the chains, at least get one wrist free so that I could use my flame against him. Eventually, he must have gotten tired of watching me, for suddenly, he was in front of me, his fingers wrapped around my throat, lifting me off the ground.

I choked, gasping for air, my eyes meeting his as he slowly squeezed the life out of me. Tears streamed down my cheeks as I kicked at him with my feet. A shoe flew off, clattering to the floor. Spots appeared in my vision, and my struggles stopped. I was dying. I couldn't believe it. Me? A vampire hunter. A fire demon. Dying at the hands of a vampire—and so damn easy, too. Like it was no effort for him at all to hold me up by the neck with one hand while I fought for breath. My eyes fluttered closed, and then, only then, did he release me.

One foot hit the floor, and I wobbled madly. Without my shoe, the other foot didn't reach the floor at all. Gasping and coughing, I sucked in a breath, trying to calm my ragged breathing, focusing on the breath that my lungs had been starved for. He watched dispassionately.

"Who are you?" It was hard to speak through my bruised throat, and I couldn't contain the wince.

"Who I am doesn't matter. The question is, who are you?" He remained in front of me. Close. Too close for comfort. I clamped my mouth shut and eyeballed him.

"Don't want to talk? That's okay, little one. I'll help you, shall I?" He leaned in so close I could feel his breath on my cheek. I shuddered. Then his face was at my neck, and he breathed in, whispering, "Delicious," and I closed my eyes. Then his mouth was on my neck, his tongue brushing over the vein that was pounding wildly, then the graze of his teeth. His fangs. Oh god. He was going to bite me. I'd never been bitten, had avoided that catastrophe all this time, but now it was my turn, and I quaked at the prospect.

"Who do you work for?" Another scrape of his teeth.

"No one." I choked, hating the fear in my voice. I wanted to be stronger than this, but I wasn't an idiot. He was an old vampire. Had to be. He had power, skills, and smarts. I'd been outwitted, and I had to applaud that. Had he played me all along? Or was it only when we arrived at the warehouse that he realized something was up?

He raised his head, leaned one hand above my head while he crowded in close. I pushed myself back against the pole I was chained to, tried to drive myself all the way through and out the other side— of course, it doesn't work like that. I was trapped.

"Bullshit. Try again. Who. Do. You. Work. For?" Each word was punctuated by his fingers inching around the back of my neck and then jerking, forcing my head to bang painfully against the pole but also giving him easier access to my artery.

"I don't work for anyone." I tried to hide my fear from him, but no doubt he could sense it leaking from me—let's not kid ourselves, it wasn't leaking; it was pouring out of me in waves. I was shit scared, and he knew it.

"Too bad. I liked you." Then he bit me. I screamed. A startled, garbled sound. Through the pain of his fangs piercing my skin, I felt him pull deeply, swallowing my blood, my life. Some sense of self-preservation kicked in, and I struggled, letting my aching wrists hold my body weight, I wrapped my legs around him and squeezed. Hard.

It kind of worked. He raised his head, his tongue sweeping across his bottom lip to capture the blood that lingered there. Screwing up my face, I squeezed my thighs even tighter. Only he wasn't reacting to my crushing grip the way I was expecting.

"That's some grip you've got," he commented, and I stopped, looking at him in shock.

"Some grip?" I practically shouted, outraged. "I've got thighs of steel, mister. You should be screaming in agony by now. Why aren't you?" I didn't know where this blast of anger came from, this rush of adrenaline, but I wasn't going to question it. I just went with it.

He threw his head back and laughed, which only served to incite me even further.

"Maybe because I'm a hundred-and-eighty-year-old vampire who's stronger than you." His humor eased, and he looked me over, his eyes focusing on my neck where I could feel the warm wetness where he'd bitten me. It continued to throb, and even though I was a fast healer, I wasn't that fast. I hoped I didn't bleed out here.

With startling ease, he reached behind, unhooked my ankles from where they only just met behind his lower back and removed my legs from their death grip around his waist.

"Not that I wasn't enjoying that…" He grinned wolfishly. "But we've got work to do."

"Work?" I wasn't following. What did he mean, work?

Stepping back, he let my legs drop, and this time I lost the other shoe. I couldn't reach the ground and dangled, my shoulders screaming, the chains biting into my wrists painfully.

"You were about to tell me who you work for." He grabbed the chair, flipped it around, straddled it, and sat, resting his forearms over the back.

"I've already told you I don't work for anyone." I tried to get a grip on the pole with my bare feet, get some traction to ease the pressure on my arms.

"I find that hard to believe. You see, yesterday I saw you being most alluring with a vampire, promising him all sorts of delights. Then you brought him here but left alone a short time later. Imagine my surprise when I found nothing left of that poor unfortunate vampire except for a dusting of ash and a pile of clothes." His eyes traveled to a drum in the corner of the warehouse where I'd been throwing the clothes and other items the vampires I'd ended had on their bodies when they'd died.

"Seems you've been doing this a while," he continued. "I counted thirteen wallets."

Fuck. Should have got rid of the evidence. What a rookie mistake, I berated myself. I'd ditched their phones, ripped out their sim cards, and snapped them in half, but everything else I'd shoved into that drum with the intent that I'd incinerate it all. I just hadn't gotten around to it yet.

"You knew him?" No point denying it. What I hadn't factored in with my hunting games was that vampires might have friends who'd come looking for them. Even worse, old, powerful friends, for the older the vampire, the stronger they were. I had a feeling I was shit out of luck.

"No." He shook his head, returning his attention to me, studying me with what appeared to be great consideration. "So, if you're not working for anyone, as you claim, why are you killing vampires? What did these men do to you?"

"They're vampires!" I cried. That was reason enough. Bloodsucking, soulless vermin.

"You're telling me you killed them purely

because they were vampires?" An eyebrow arched, and his eyes took on a cold, hard intensity.

"Yes." I was about to die. I could see it in his face. And if our positions were reversed, I would do the same. Kill the asshole who'd been killing my species. If someone were killing fire demons just because they were fire demons, I'd be pissed too.

"You're facing quite the dilemma, aren't you?" What did he mean, a dilemma? I frowned, confused.

"I guess I should introduce myself." He stood, approached me again, and I couldn't help the flinch in response to his nearness. "My name is Nate Wilder, and I'm the Director of the Supernatural Investigation Agency."

"SIA." Of course, I'd heard of the SIA. Agent Jordan Buchanan had come to town to deal with our vampire problem, recruited my cousin Rae, and then buggered off with the job half done. "And what, exactly, is my dilemma?"

"Vigilante actions such as yours are what the SIA is here to stop. You're breaking the law, and I'm going to have to take you in."

"What? You're arresting me?" I couldn't believe it. The vampires were the problem here, not me!

"You're killing vampires who have done nothing

wrong. They are, believe it or not, innocent. You've gone rogue."

I stared at him in absolute shock. Oh, my God. Was he right? Had I turned into a monster myself? No. It couldn't be. I was fighting the vampire problem in Maxxan; I was helping.

"They're not innocent," I protested. "I'm helping to rid Maxxan of the epidemic sweeping through our town."

"Epidemic?" His brows rose. "Hardly. With the deadnettle crops gone, and the operation dismantled, that element has cleared out, searching for somewhere else to set up shop. Maxxan is no longer viable for them."

"But the Gunslinger...we have to find the Gunslinger."

"The Gunslinger has gone underground. That's his MO, and he's good at it. The sighting of him here is the first in years—he operates under the radar and has a loyal team protecting him. We'll continue our search for him, but he is not our top priority."

"Who is?"

"A rogue on the loose in Maxxan murdering vampires."

The silence that followed was deafening. *I was the bad guy.* I dangled from the chains, my head spinning, taking in what he'd said. I'd been killing innocent vampires—was that why my investigation had stalled? Because my targets weren't real targets, they were vampires, and I assumed they were involved because of their species. Closing my eyes, I reeled from the reality of it. I was the rogue. I was the criminal. I was wanted. I was a murderer.

"What's going to happen to me?" I whispered, blinking to keep the moisture that was welling up in my eyes from overflowing.

"You'll be taken to SIA HQ in Redmeadows, where you'll be held until sentencing."

My heart stopped. I was sure of it. My breathing stopped, too, at least until my lungs were screaming for oxygen, and only then did I suck in a breath. This couldn't be happening. Panic swept through me. How had I gotten this so wrong? I'd been so sure, so full of pride and confidence in my actions. There had to be another way; I had to be able to get out of this. I just had to think—which was near impossible with my shoulders about to pop out of my sockets at any moment.

I couldn't let him arrest me. I was panicked and grasping at straws when it hit me. A deal! I'd offer him a deal.

"How about this..." I cleared my throat, pushed

down the quiver, and straightened my spine. "We fight for it. Winner takes all."

"Fight?" he queried.

"Yes. You and me. Hand-to-hand combat."

"Winner takes all?" That had gotten his interest; his head tilted to one side as if he were actually considering it. I nodded enthusiastically, my plan solidifying in my mind.

"Yes. If you win, you arrest me, lock me away." I shuddered at the thought.

"And if you win?" He walked around the pole, disappearing from view.

"If I win...you let me go. With no record of this."

"I think you're very clever and are trying to trick me," he drawled right by my ear, making me jump. "Winner takes all means a fight to the death. If you win, that means I'm dead. And vice versa."

Damn it. He had me. But I was sure I could take him if I weren't chained to this damn pole.

"However, I accept your terms. Winner takes all it is." The chains dropped, and I fell to the floor on my hands and knees. He'd been behind me, but when I glanced over my shoulder, he wasn't there. Calling forth my power, I balanced a fireball in one hand to illuminate the warehouse. Damn it, where was he?

I spotted him across the warehouse, cracking his knuckles and rolling his head around his shoulders in preparation. His eyes flashed, and I threw my first fireball. He moved so fast I couldn't track him, and the fireball hit the wall, entirely missing its target. Okay. Regrouping, I forced myself to focus. No more fireballs. I'd burn the warehouse down at this rate. Lasso, it was. Conjuring my lasso in one hand and a dagger in the other, I bent my knees and swiveled, searching for him once more.

A whisper of air to my left had me swinging blindly, but I failed to connect. He stopped a few feet away and grinned at me, his fingers beckoning. I charged, lasso swinging, dagger gripped tight, ready to slash at him. This time he didn't move away, and I let out a roar. My lasso was almost to him when he grabbed hold of it and ripped it out of my grip. As soon as my connection with it was lost, it fizzled into nothing. Damn it, how had he done that? I could easily conjure another one, but if he could deal with it so quickly, I needed to rethink my approach. Instead, I summoned a sword and swung. He raised an arm to block, and I swiped low with my dagger, dragging it across his thigh. In return, he delivered a hard and painful kick to my stomach. I flew through the air, landed with a crash, and slid along the floor until I hit the far wall of the warehouse. *Ouch.*

Scrambling to my feet, breathing slowly, and trying to ignore the pain in my stomach, I approached again. He met me head-on. Each attempt to slice him with my dagger or sword resulted in a punch to the head, shoulder, stomach, wherever he could reach. I was reeling, seeing stars, for his blows rained on me, heavily and rapidly. I spat out blood from his latest blow and dragged myself onto my hands and knees. I was outclassed in hand-to-hand combat with him, but pride would not let me admit defeat. And the prospect of being arrested, the shame I'd bring to my family, was too much to bear. I had to win this or die trying.

I sprang to my feet and charged. There was another blur of motion, and then he was on me. I blocked blow after blow and tried to get in some of my own—hitting the mark occasionally but never finding his heart.

I was dripping sweat, spitting blood, and shaking uncontrollably. I was pretty sure I was dying, but determined to give it one last shot. I lunged, sword aimed at his chest. He deflected and punched me again, a devastating blow that threw me high into the air and had me crashing to the floor with a loud crack. Pretty sure he'd just broken my spine. I was a ball of pain; blood was pooling in my throat, making it hard to breathe. I turned my head to spit it out, but it merely trickled from my lips. I watched him approach dully, my eyes swollen and everything tinted red. *I was dying.* This wasn't how I thought I'd go out.

He stood over me, a booted foot on each side of my hips, looking at me dispassionately. Just do it! I screamed in my head because I couldn't speak, couldn't nod, couldn't move. End it. End me. End this.

Then I passed out.

I AWOKE WITH A START, shooting upwards so fast my head spun. One thing was blatantly obvious—I was no longer in the warehouse. In fact, I was in bed. A big, luxurious bed. One I'd never seen before, and I was stark naked. Snatching the sheet to my chest, I looked around, my heart hammering in my chest. Where was I, and what the hell was going on?

"You're awake." Rotating my head, I saw the vampire I'd just been given an absolute hiding by, heading my way, naked except for a towel slung around his hips. His hair was wet, and the door he'd just come through stood open behind him, steam wafting out, indicating a bathroom.

I slid off the far side of the bed, dragging the sheet with me, putting as much distance between us as I could.

"What? Now you're afraid?" he said, stopping to study me. I couldn't drag my eyes from him, again taken aback by the physical perfection, the taut abs, the expanse of flesh that made me want to run my fingers over it. A tribal tattoo curved over one shoulder and around the bicep of his arm. His skin wasn't the pasty white of other vampires; he had a tanned, olive complexion with a smattering of hair leading from his belly button to below the towel. I quickly dragged my eyes back up to his, which were now dark.

"You're going to want to stop looking at me like that," he warned. "You might not like the consequences."

"Consequences?" I squeaked; my brain flooded with my unexpected arousal. I hadn't stopped to examine the fact that I wasn't in pain, that my spine wasn't broken, that I was still alive.

"You want me to fuck you?" It was crude, but my stomach quivered at the thought. I couldn't seriously believe I was contemplating it. Sleep with a vampire? Never. Over my dead body. Which brought us back to me not being dead.

"Why aren't I dead?" I turned my back, focused on tucking the sheet more firmly around myself, anything to keep my mind—and eyes—off him.

"I healed you." His response was bland. Offhand. As if he couldn't care less that I was standing mere feet away, naked, a confused bundle of emotions and hormones.

"How?" Why did I bother asking? I already knew what the answer was. My fingers crept up to my neck and pressed. I blew out a breath of relief when I found a pulse. He hadn't turned me.

"You know about our blood?" He'd been watching me, saw me check my pulse. I shrugged. I'd learned a few things from the vampires I'd interrogated. One of them was that their blood could heal humans. That was how they kept blood slaves alive. It couldn't, however, resurrect a human if a vampire accidentally killed one, but it could bring you back from the brink of death.

"You didn't intend to kill me at all, did you?" If he had wanted me dead, he wouldn't have toyed with me like he did, dragging our fight out, hurting me. Oh no, if it was death he wanted, he would have been sure, fast, effective, of that I was positive.

His shrug told me all I needed to know.

"Why?"

"I wanted to see what you could do." I watched as he crossed to where a suitcase sat open. He rummaged inside and tossed some black fabric at me without turning. Automatically I caught it, one hand clutching the slipping sheet to my neck.

"Put that on." Paying zero attention to me, he dropped his towel, and I squeezed my eyes shut to block out the view of his tight, naked ass.

"You have about three seconds before I turn around," he warned. "You may want to put that shirt on before that happens."

Right. I quickly pulled the T-shirt over my head. It was way too big, of course, but it covered more than some of my dresses did. Once clothed, I shimmied the sheet out from under the shirt and tossed it on the bed.

In the time it had taken me to pull on one single T-shirt, he was fully dressed in jeans, a shirt, and a leather jacket, all black. On his belt was clipped a red shield. SIA.

"Aren't you hot?" I asked, indicating the jacket. Although the hotel room we were in was air-conditioned, it was far from cold enough to need a coat.

"Vampires don't feel the heat. Or cold."

"Oh." Smoothing my palms down the hem of the borrowed shirt that reached just above my knees, I asked the question I didn't want to ask but had to know the answer, regardless.

"What now?"

He cocked his head, studying me. I couldn't read his expression at all, and I swallowed the uncomfortable lump in my throat. Was he going to arrest me? Lock me away in the SIA cells in Redmeadows with my Uncle Frank? According to him, I deserved it, but I couldn't bring myself to regret my actions. Vampires were evil. Point me at a vampire, and I'll try to kill it, for, at one time or another, they'd done something to deserve it. I didn't buy for one second that those that I had killed were innocent.

"You mean our little wager?" He smirked, his eyes running from the top of my head to the tip of my toes and back again. "It means I own you now."

"What?" And just like that, my temper went from zero to one hundred in a split second. "Listen here, asshole, no one owns me. No one. I'd rather rot in jail than be your property." Later I'd probably regret my rash words, but in the heat of the moment, they fell out of my mouth unheeded.

"You're reneging on our agreement?" His voice was cold, his eyes hard. I swallowed. "It was you, was it not, who challenged me? Hand-to-hand combat, winner take all?"

"It was," I admitted, my anger fleeing as quickly as it had arrived.

"Would you prefer I let you die?" he persisted. I hesitated. Did I wish I were dead rather than be indebted to him? It seemed he took my silence as a yes, for before I could blink, his fingers wrapped around my throat, and I was propelled back against the wall with my feet dangling in the air once more.

"I can remedy that, Spitfire," he said, uncaring that I couldn't breathe, that I dangled helplessly in his grip. How could he be so cold? Oh right. He was a vampire. Clearly, my brain wasn't functioning at its normal level after all the lack of oxygen it had experienced since meeting him. "But you have too much spirit to want to die." He lowered me to the floor and loosened his hold slightly, enough to let a thin stream of oxygen into my lungs. I clutched at his wrist with both hands but couldn't break his grip.

"I won—winner takes all. Agreed?"

I nodded. He had me fair and square. I'd challenged him and lost, and as much as it pained me to admit it, he was right. Now I was wishing that I hadn't been so rash with my words, that I'd put some stipulations around the definition of winner takes all, for the images dancing through my head had me trembling. Would he turn me into his blood slave, drink from me until I was on the verge of death, only to heal me and do the whole thing over and over again? Or maybe it was sex he was after. Or both. I shuddered at the thought.

He laughed, and I stiffened at the unexpected sound. "You are as transparent as a sheet of glass, Spitfire." He rubbed his thumb along my jaw, and I ignored the shiver that followed. I would not enjoy a caress from a vampire, I told myself.

"What do you want?" I ground out, trying to jerk my head back.

"Not what you think." He released me, and I almost sagged to the floor in relief. "I never force myself on a woman, ever. You want me, then all you have to do is ask. It would be my pleasure."

Blood rushed to my cheeks, and I dragged my eyes from him to the window, seeing nothing as the heavy curtains blocked the light. I didn't even know if it was day or night, how long I'd been here, or just exactly what had gone on before I woke.

"I won't be asking." I bristled and then froze when he lowered his head, his lips hovering mere millimeters from mine.

"Oh, you will. You can bet on it," he whispered. Then he was gone, nothing but a blur, until he stopped on the other side of the room.

"I won't kill you or arrest you, provided you help me," he said.

"Help you? How?" I was curious. How could I possibly help a vampire?

"All in good time. If you want to leave this room a free woman, I need your agreement. If not,"—he touched his fingers to the badge on his belt—"then I'm more than happy to arrange accommodations at the SIA for you."

He had me. Help him or go to jail.

"Fine. I'll help," I grumbled. I was between a rock and a hard place, and he knew it, the bastard.

"Good." He strode toward me, steps purposeful, and it was all I could do to hold my ground and not step backward, away from his commanding presence. He held out a hand. I looked at it and slowly placed my palm against his—a handshake to seal the deal. I had a sinking feeling I was going to regret this.

"What's the plan?" I asked, pulling my hand from his and absently wiping my palm against my outer thigh.

"You need to trust me," he said, his eyes not missing a thing.

"It's not that easy!" I cried, throwing both hands in the air. "You can't just shake on a deal and say trust me and expect me to trust you!"

"Fair enough, Spitfire." He inclined his head. "We both have to learn to trust each other. I have to trust that you will not plunge a flaming sword through my heart at the first opportunity that presents itself, and you will have to trust that I will not go back on my word."

Hugging my arms around myself, I began pacing. I was in over my head but confident I could find my way out of this. A loophole. Something. I would not be indebted to a vampire, not if I could help it. And whatever it was he wanted my help with, he was very cagey about it. Was it illegal? Something that would get him in trouble with his precious SIA? Wait! Hadn't he said he was the director of the SIA? What was the director doing here in Maxxan? Shouldn't this be something for one of his agents?

"It's exhausting watching you think, Spitfire," he grumbled. Stalking to the bed, he shook a pillow loose from its case and disappeared into the bathroom, returning moments later and holding the pillowcase out to me.

"What's this?" I eyed it suspiciously, for it was now bulging.

"Your clothes. I'm not sure if they are salvageable." I took the pillowcase from him and peeked inside to see my leather pants, top, and shoes. All reeked of blood. Mine. I mourned the loss of the clothes and shoes. They had been expensive, and I'd have to save up to replace them.

"I doubt it." Flashes of the beating I'd taken at his hand played through my mind, the pain, the utter feeling of helplessness at the end when I was dying. I vowed he would never make me feel that way again.

As I held the pillowcase, the blood started to leak through, red stains appearing on the white fabric. I wrinkled my nose in distaste, then, hearing his sudden intake of breath, I focused my attention on him. He could smell my blood, and judging by the darkening of his eyes and descending fangs, he liked what he smelled.

"I am not your food." Stalking to the wastebasket, I dropped the bundle inside.

"You are whatever I need you to be. Remember?" His drawl was infuriating, but when he grabbed my wrist and tugged me toward him, I was taken aback by the coldness in his eyes. "I won. We have a deal. I have already told you I will not force myself upon you—in any way—but heed my words, Spitfire— you will do as I say."

"Or what?" I challenged.

"Or face the consequences."

"Which are?" *Oh my God, why couldn't I shut up?* His eyes flashed, showing his anger, and I knew I was pushing him, but I couldn't stop myself.

"Let's hope you don't find out," was his response before he dropped my wrist and strode to the door, flinging it open. It was dark out.

"How long have I been here?"

"A day." He gestured for me to follow, and barefoot, wearing nothing but a T-shirt, I did.

"People will be looking for me." I followed him to my car. He'd obviously used it to transport us both back to the hotel last night. If anyone recognized it, they could only assume I'd spent the night with a man at a seedy hotel. Great. Not that I had a pure virgin reputation in Maxxan, but no need to add fuel to the fire.

"No one is looking for you," he assured me. "I have your phone." He held it up—I hadn't even seen him remove it from his jacket.

"What the hell? Give that back." I tried to snatch it from him, but he held it out of reach, grinning at my attempts to jump up and retrieve it.

"Asshole," I said under my breath, knowing he'd hear me.

"Drive," was his only response, tossing me the keys.

"You trust me to drive?" I asked, surprised.

"Better to keep you occupied and behind the wheel than a passenger planning on running me through with one of her flaming weapons," he replied drolly. It was infuriating that he had me pegged, damn it.

I slid behind the wheel and slammed the door, jumping when he appeared in the passenger seat next to me. Man, he was fast.

"Where to?" I asked, starting the car and automatically putting it into reverse.

"Your place."

I froze, then turned my head, pinning him with a look. "My place?"

"You need to change. Unless you want to walk around looking like that? Not your usual standard, I'm sure."

Goddamn it, he had me again. Without a word, I reversed, swung the car wide, and moved into drive, peeling away from the hotel with a screech of tires.

As we drove, my mind was working furiously on a plan. Vampires couldn't enter your home unless invited. So, by taking me to my apartment, he was doing me a favor. I could get inside, away from him, where he couldn't control me. I just had to wait out the night, for with the Red Witch lifting the spell that allowed vampires to walk in the daylight, come sunrise, he'd fry.

There was a small parking lot at the rear of the bakery where staff—and I—could park and a staircase outside the building leading directly to my apartment. Feeling him right behind me, breathing on my neck, I climbed up, trying not to wince at the grated metal of the stairs biting into my bare feet. At the door, I had my key in the lock when his hand gripped the doorknob, holding it shut.

"Don't think I haven't thought of that." His voice

was low, and he was incredibly close, his body lightly touching mine from hip to shoulder.

"I don't know what you mean," I lied.

"Invite me in." It wasn't a request. It was an order. I couldn't. I couldn't do it. If I invited him in once, that was it—he would forever have access to my home. I couldn't un-invite him.

"No." I kept my eyes on the door mere inches from my face, felt him stiffen behind me, then press closer.

His next words were breathed directly in my ear, and I shivered. "Is there anyone you hold dear in this building? Because you, and you alone, will be responsible for what happens next if you do not invite me in. I will set this place ablaze and kill them all—and that will be on you."

I swallowed, thinking of the staff working in the bakery. Kay, the owner with her plump figure and pink cheeks, Shaun, the apprentice baker who was so painfully shy he stuttered every time I said hello to him, Martha, the waitress who flirted with everyone, male and female alike, and earned her body weight in tips because of it.

"You wouldn't!"

"Try me."

I couldn't risk it, and he knew it, the bastard. He

had me. Studying my toes with great concentration, I whispered, "Come in."

I didn't know what I was expecting, a flash of lightning, the sparkling of magic, something at least to mark this momentous occasion, but nothing happened. Nothing changed. He merely twisted the doorknob and pushed the door open, ushering me inside with a hand against my back.

I stepped inside, and he followed. He was in my home. My refuge. I was no longer safe here. I wasn't safe anywhere anymore, and it rattled me more than I ever thought it would. I was screwed.

FOUR

"Nice place," he commented, the sheer size of him dwarfing my tiny living space. He moved to the window, peered out to the street below, then turned and headed back to the door.

"Where are you going?"

He looked at me over his shoulder. "Why? Want me to stay?" One brow rose, and his gaze held mine for a long moment.

"As if." Crossing my arms over my chest, I frowned. "Why insist on being invited in if you didn't actually want to be here?"

"You're not that naïve," he drawled. "Get some rest. I'll be back later; we've got work to do."

I opened my mouth to ask what work, but he was gone, the door closing silently behind him. And then the shock set in. The devastating truth that I was now beholden to a vampire, and he had free access to my home. The very vermin I despised and had made it my work to destroy. Here. In my home.

Sinking onto the sofa, I cradled my head in my hands and stared blindly at the carpet, my mind whirling. What to do next? I had to do something. I couldn't sit here and wait for his return. I held my hands out in front of me, the chipped nail polish and two broken nails a blatant reminder of the challenge I'd lost.

In the kitchen, I pulled an opened bottle of wine from the fridge and poured myself a glass, gulping it down, before refilling the glass and repeating the action. The hit of alcohol helped. Not enough to wipe out the recent events, but enough to ease the shaking. Carrying the glass with me to the bathroom, I examined myself in the mirror. What a red-hot mess. My hair was hanging past my shoulders in a tangled mess, dried blood congealing the knots together. My face bore remnants of blood smears, and my makeup was now streaked down my cheeks, my lipstick smeared around my mouth. I looked like a depressed, suicidal clown.

I was about to flick on the shower when it hit me. What was I thinking? I couldn't stay here; I couldn't be here when he got back! And even though it went against everything I believed about myself, I vetoed repairing my appearance in favor of getting the hell out of Dodge. Rushing into the bedroom, I grabbed a suitcase and began throwing clothes in, then back to the bathroom, where I swiped the contents of the counter into my toiletries bag with no regard for their welfare. My heart rate picked up, sweat beaded my skin as an overwhelming sense of panic settled over me. If this was my flight or fight response kicking in, I was firmly in the flight corner.

Wearing nothing but the T-shirt he'd given me, I dragged my suitcase to the door, returned to retrieve my Kate Spade leather satchel that doubled as my purse, and slid my laptop into it. Then I flung open the door.

"Going somewhere?" Nate Wilder stood on my doorstep, one hand against the doorframe. I couldn't contain the squeal that slipped out. With a sigh, he straightened and placed a hand against my chest, gently pushing me back inside. I almost cried when the door clicked ominously behind him, shutting us in my apartment.

"I—" I didn't know what to say, for once lost for words. I was so busted.

"Perhaps I didn't make myself clear earlier?" Crossing his arms over his chest, he eyeballed me.

I snorted. Was he serious? Apparently, he was, for he watched me with solemn eyes, his face unreadable. I couldn't tell if he was angry, disappointed, or somewhere in between.

"I panicked." It was the truth. As soon as he'd left my apartment, panic had set in. I shifted my weight from one foot to the other, saw him track the movement, and made myself stop. He was reading my body language, understanding me, and I had a feeling he was damn good at it. He nodded, and it took every ounce of willpower I had not to back away when his big body stood in front of me. I stared hard at his chest, refusing to meet his eyes.

"Let me make myself perfectly clear," he began, no inflection whatsoever in his voice. "We have an agreement. One I expect you to uphold. If you run, if you try to wriggle out of it, I will hunt you down. I have more resources than you can ever imagine. You don't like me? I don't care; you're going to like SIA lockup a lot less."

I sucked in a breath. "You'd still arrest me?"

"Don't give me cause to. I'm prepared to uphold my end of the bargain, but I'm adding an addendum. You will help me, and you will not run." Oh, he was brilliant, the bastard. Fear and anger combined, mingling through my blood like a hazy cocktail, heating me, sizzling in intensity. A spark of electricity danced across my knuckles. Of course, he didn't miss a thing. His hand completely enveloped mine, my clenched fist tucked inside his palm, his fingers wrapped tight around mine.

"You have talent." His voice was so low I had to strain to hear. "But you lack discipline. You react instinctively, without thought. That is what is going to get you killed."

"You're going to kill me?" I squeaked. Since he hadn't done so when he had the opportunity, I'd naively thought I was off the hook in that regard.

"Not me. You have it in your head that vampires are the bad guys, Paige Shelton, when you need to open your eyes and see what is happening around you."

"What?" I was confused. What was happening around me? He shook his head, released my fist, and began pacing backward and forward along the length of the room.

"How do you know my name?" I zeroed in on

him using my name. He cast me a you've-got-to-be-kidding look.

"License plates. Address. Ran it through the database. Not exactly difficult."

I mulled it over. It made sense. He had the entire SIA at his disposal. Finding out someone's identity would be a piece of cake for someone like him.

"Surely you didn't expect me to accept your rules meekly?" I said, changing tack.

To my surprise, he laughed. "Anything but, Spitfire." Suddenly he was in front of me, propelling me back until I fell on the sofa, trapped with his arms on either side of my head, all humor gone. "We had an agreement. I was under the impression you were an honorable person. Am I mistaken?"

He hit me where it hurt, and I winced. I put a lot of pride in honoring my word, and he hit the nail on the head. I had agreed to his terms, never mind that I hadn't wanted to, never mind that it had been my own stupid fault for getting myself into such a situation in the first place.

"Sorry," I muttered, closing my eyes to avoid looking at him.

"I don't want your apology," he ground out. "I want your word. You agreed to help me in return for your freedom. Does that still stand?"

"Yes," I whispered.

"Look at me." His frustration was evident. Reluctantly, I opened my eyes and looked directly into his. The gray swirled like a stormy night, darkening at the edges. They were really quite mesmerizing. A shiver danced over my skin when his fingers curled along my jaw. I couldn't look away even if I wanted to.

"Do. We. Have. A. Deal?" I knew this was the last time he'd ask me, that if he didn't like my answer, I was going to find myself in cuffs in an SIA cell. And I had agreed. No matter that I wished I hadn't, I had, and I was a woman whose word meant something.

"We have a deal," I whispered.

"You won't try to renege? Wriggle out of it? Run?" he pressed.

"Why do you need my help so badly?" Some of my fight was coming back, for it occurred to me that the grip he had along my jaw was gentle, almost a caress, and his eyes were anything but hard.

"Answer me first." His eyes moved to my mouth, and I couldn't help but run my tongue along my lower lip. What the hell was I doing? It seemed he wanted to know, too, for he moved closer still, his mouth a hairsbreadth from mine. "And don't think seducing me will get you out of this. I will take what you offer, but nothing will change." My breath hitched. The way he said "take" had my stomach clenching, and a tingling I hadn't felt in a long time started low in my abdomen. I almost groaned at the irony of it all. Me, a vampire slayer, attracted to the very creature I hunted.

"You have my word—I will not run or try to get out of our deal." As soon as the words left my mouth, he kissed me. Hard. And then he was standing on the opposite side of the room, watching me with hooded eyes as I dazedly touched my fingers to my lips.

"What was that?" I breathed, dazed at the turn of events.

"Surely you don't need me to explain?" he mocked, arms once again crossed. "The way you dress, the way you move, tells me you're a hot-blooded woman who's had her share of kisses."

"The way I dress? Seriously? You want to go down that road?"

"Nah. I just played that back in my head, and I sound like a dick."

His admission and self-deprecating humor threw me.

"Relax. It was just a kiss," he said.

"Seriously?" I sputtered, torn between liking this

big, badass, sexy as fucking sin vampire and wanting to kill him.

"Seriously. And I warned you that trying to seduce me would change nothing. Except, of course, we'd be having hot sex."

Images flashed in my mind of exactly how hot the sex would be with Nate Wilder. I swallowed, acknowledging I was in over my head with this vampire. He made me feel things I did not want to feel; he made me question my own judgment and decisions, and I didn't like it.

"Back to my question." I cleared my throat and crossed my arms over my chest, mimicking his pose. "Why do you need my help?"

"There is someone in Maxxan that I need to track down. Only he can sense me a mile off. I need someone to run interference for me, to distract him and lure him out of hiding without him being any the wiser."

"I'm bait." I huffed, affronted.

"Spitfire, you've been using yourself as bait to lure those vampires to your warehouse. This is nothing different."

"Fine. Then what? You want me to lure this vampire to my warehouse, and then?"

"Then I interrogate him." He shrugged, as if the answer was obvious. Which I supposed it was.

"So, this someone…is a big deal?" They had to be if he was after them, but he surprised me by shaking his head.

"There are no high rollers in Maxxan, but he has information that will be useful to my investigation."

"What investigation?"

"Classified." His lips quirked when I huffed.

A headache was forming behind my eyes, and I squeezed the bridge of my nose.

"Are you all right?" It couldn't be concern I heard in his voice, not coming from a blood-sucking vampire. "You're a little pale."

"I'm fine." I got to my feet, ignoring the wave of dizziness that swept over me. I was tired, that's all. I angled my head toward the door. "You can go. I promised I wouldn't run, and I won't. But I'd like to get cleaned up and get some rest."

He studied me intently for a moment before nodding his head. "I'll see you at sunset tomorrow."

"I'll be here," I promised.

The door closed, and finally, I felt like I could breathe. Retrieving my laptop from its bag, I set it back up on my desk and logged in, all the while thinking about Nate Wilder, how he'd moved, the speed and strength he had. It was my own fault that I'd been beaten so thoroughly. I hadn't researched my prey, had thought that because I'd successfully taken down over a dozen vampires, he would be no different. But I'd overlooked something significant. He was SIA. He had training. Elite training. And although I was well-schooled in self-defense, it didn't compare, not even remotely.

I typed his name in the internet browser. What appeared on my screen surprised me, and I read with round eyes.

Nate was one wealthy vampire. He owned several properties in Redmeadows, including the Crimson Mist nightclub. He lived in the Garden District in a big old mansion, no less. Of course, the results didn't allude to his species status. Vampire. Jordan had drummed into all of us that the number one rule of the Supernatural Investigation Agency was to keep the public unaware of paranormals. Only those who needed to know knew.

My research ended with photo after photo of Nate with a stream of beautiful women hanging off his arm. I stared hard at the images on my screen and couldn't deny Nate Wilder was as handsome as fuck. He was also a womanizer, judging by the photos. He was rarely seen with the same woman twice, and I wondered if these women were merely food for him.

Slamming down the lid of the laptop, I ran my fingers through my hair, only to be halted by the dried blood still trapped amongst the strands. Damn it, I was a mess. In the bathroom, I flicked on the tap in the shower—I was long overdue.

FIVE

Surprisingly, I slept through the rest of the night and most of the following morning, not stirring until my cell phone dinged, indicating a text message.

"Delivery for you, hun." It was from downstairs. My online purchases were delivered to the bakery, and I felt a little quiver of anticipation. I was expecting my Yves Saint Laurent facial cream today.

"Thanks, sweetie. I'll be down soon," I typed back. Then smiled. This felt normal. This was the life I was used to. Had everything that had happened with Nate been a bad dream? Laughing to myself, I slid out of bed. Doubtful. His commanding presence was too intense for any dream. As I'd drifted off to sleep last night, my mind had been fixated on one thing—how could I possibly find a vampire attractive? We'd been brought up thinking all vampires were evil. But this man, this vampire... I had a sneaking suspicion he was honorable. After all, he was the Director of the SIA. They wouldn't let an asshole take that position, surely? Although, considering human politics, who knew?

Dressing in a white cotton eyelet Dolce and Gabbana maxi dress, I braided my hair over one shoulder, applied my usual day-wear makeup, slid my feet into a pair of Saint Laurent sandals, and skipped downstairs to get my package. Outside, the sun was shining, another stinking hot day in Maxxan, and tilting my face to the sun, I smiled. Fire demons love the heat, and I was no exception. I toyed with taking a trip out to Grandma's old house, now Rae's, and running around naked in the sunlight, just to recharge, but work beckoned. If I wanted to keep myself well stocked in designer clothes—and I did—then I needed to get my fingers to the keyboard and bring in more clients. Too bad the vampire hunting business didn't pay.

The lunch crowd had thinned in the bakery, and I only had to wait a few minutes to be served. I never collected a package without buying something; it was an ingrained habit. Today I'd chosen an iced tea and a muffin and settled myself at a seat near the window to wait for my order. That was when I heard them. Two teenage boys, whispering to each other, only they were loud whispers. I could easily listen to what they were saying, and to say I was concerned was an understatement.

"You got them?" one asked.

There was a rustling, then the other replied, "Yeah! Enough for two girls. One each." There was a smile in that voice, an indication they were pleased with whatever it was they had purchased.

"Who should we give them to?"

"I reckon Shannon. She's so fucking hot, man, yet she won't even look at me. Bitch. I'm gonna fuck her up. You?"

"Becky. I've always liked her."

I sucked in a breath and held it, not liking where my imagination was going. I didn't hear right, did I? They weren't planning on drugging these girls, were they?

"They're coming tonight, aren't they?" voice one asked, sounding a little hesitant, a little unsure.

"Defo. Got word from Jarrod. Practically the whole senior year will be there. Make sure you wear a condom, bro. Don't want to get the damn bitch pregnant."

I almost sniggered out loud. So, they figured it was okay to drug and rape a girl, but don't get her pregnant?

I'd been listening so intently that I jumped when Kay slid my order in front of me. I thanked her, taking the opportunity to turn and see who the teenage boys were, to see if I knew them, but their table was now empty. Damn.

"Hey." I stopped Kay before she moved away. "Is there a party tonight? Teenagers?"

"Oh yeah, it's all the young uns have been talking about all week. Jarrod Reed's folks are out of town, and they're having a pool party. Don't worry, the sheriff has already been alerted, and he's promised to do a drive-by to check up on 'em, keep them out of too much mischief."

"The Reeds.... out on Watermill Road?"

"Yeah, that's the place. Why? You thinking of going?" Kay laughed, and I joined in.

"Nah. Just curious. I remember when Jarrod was in diapers. Hard to think of him at high school and throwing parties."

"He's seventeen now. A real looker too." Kay wiped down the table next to me, then hustled back to the counter, leaving me to ponder what to do about what I'd overheard. I didn't know who the two boys were, and I wasn't one hundred percent sure they intended to drug the girls, but it sure sounded that way, and I could not let that happen.

While I ate my muffin and drank my iced tea, I pulled up the internet on my phone and began researching Maxxan High School, following the link to social media and taking a stab at who Shannon and Becky were. Of course, there were three Rebecca's, but only one Shannon. She was a pretty blonde with blue eyes, and I'd bet she was up there as one of the most popular girls at school. Becky, though, was going to be trickier to find. Looked like I'd have to check out the party in person and see if I could identify who the two boys were and teach them a lesson they wouldn't forget in a hurry.

With a plan formulating in my mind, I hurried back upstairs. There were a few hours to kill before I headed out. I usually didn't hunt humans, but I was prepared to make an exception tonight. And I'd start early. Teenage high school kids were bound to hit the drink early and wipe out before midnight. I needed to stop that from happening.

I spent the afternoon finishing off the graphic design jobs I had pending and posting another ad online to hustle for more business. The excellent thing about being a graphic designer was that I could accept clients from anywhere in the world. If I were reliant on the small pool of contenders in Maxxan, my business would have gone under before it had begun.

Just before seven, I stood in my underwear, matching, of course, flipping through my wardrobe. Tonight wasn't about sex appeal. Tonight was about stopping two little shits from becoming utter assholes. And two girls from a traumatic experience that would haunt them for the rest of their lives. I settled on ripped jeans—Armani—and a flag print T-shirt—also Armani. I vetoed heels for Nikes. Leaving my hair in its braid over my shoulder, I quickly touched up my makeup, slid my cell phone into my back pocket, and grabbed my keys. Time to party!

THE PARTY WAS in full swing when I pulled up at the curb outside of the Reeds' house, even though the sun had only just gone down. Cars were parked the entire length of the street, and I shuddered to think how many drunk kids were going to get behind the wheel tonight. Maybe I'd do the rounds and confiscate everyone's keys.

Slamming the car door, I headed up the path. Dixie cups littered the front path, and I frowned. It looked like this party had been going on for some time already. My suspicions were confirmed when I pushed open the front door without knocking. Loud music assaulted my eardrums; chaos assaulted my eyeballs.

Girls danced in the lounge room, waving their arms in the air, drinks spilling as they giggled and twirled and eyed the boys. The boys, in turn, were dragging on cigarettes, swigging whiskey straight from the bottle, and, I assumed, doing their best to look cool. Shaking my head, I wove my way through the crowd. The boys I'd overheard this afternoon had been right. Looked like the entire bloody school was here. Dodging groping hands and ignoring wolf whistles, I squeezed my way through the lounge room, through the kitchen, and around to the den. It was impossible to identify anyone's voice amongst all the racket.

I'd done three laps of the entire house, upstairs and down, and was on the verge of giving up when I heard him. Closing my eyes, I zeroed in on his voice.

"You okay, Shannon? Looks like someone has had too much to drink." A laugh, some shuffling, then, "Why not lie down on one of the beds upstairs, sleep it off for a bit? You'll feel better."

"Yeah. Okay." Waiting in the hallway, my eyes zeroed in on a brown-haired boy, skinny with acne on his cheeks, his arm supporting the pretty blonde I'd seen online. Shannon. This was it. He'd already slipped whatever it was into her drink by the looks of things. She was all over the place, leaning heavily on him to keep herself upright, her eyes glazed. He had to get her upstairs fast for his plan to work before she passed out completely and someone came to her aid. Someone who didn't intend to rape her. What he didn't know was that someone was already here.

Stepping forward, I blocked his path, and he frowned at me with angry eyes.

"Hey. Out of the way. My girl isn't feeling well. She needs to lie down."

"Not with you, she doesn't." Tilting Shannon's head up, I peered into her unfocused eyes. "Honey," I said to her, "do you know this boy?"

"Ish Cory. Blanard," she slurred.

"Is he your boyfriend?" I pushed. She shook her head, no.

"Do you want to go upstairs? With him?"

"Listen up, bitch," Cory spat, furious I was spoiling his fun. "She's with me. Fuck off."

"You listen up, mother-fucker," I growled, nose to nose with him, my anger greater than his, my voice telling him I'd tear him to shreds and leave him bleeding at my feet. "I know you drugged this girl and intend to rape her. How about a little role reversal, huh? How would you like to feel helpless, at the mercy of someone else?" Pulling Shannon away from him with one hand, I grabbed him with the other, shooting a bolt of electricity from my body to his. He seized immediately, his body shaking and vibrating as he fell to the floor and twitched. A puddle of moisture stained the front of his pants where he'd pissed himself.

Shannon giggled, then slumped against me. Wrapping an arm around her waist, I dragged her outside to my car, settled her on the back seat, and locked her in while I went back to find the other girl, Becky. I hoped I wasn't too late.

Cory Blanard was still on the floor when I came back in, throwing off the effects of the electric shock I'd given him. A crowd had gathered, not knowing what had happened but pointing and laughing at his wet pants. He scrambled to his feet and bolted out the front door. I let him go. I hoped his experience tonight would be a lesson learned.

My frustration grew as I searched the house for the other boy, stopping to listen, trying to pinpoint anything untoward. It wasn't until I was on my third lap upstairs that I thought I heard something from behind a closed door.

"Lift your hips. Fuck, help at least a little." Someone grunted. Was it the same voice that I'd heard earlier in the day? "Come on, bitch!" Angrier now, and what sounded like a slap? Okay, drugged girl or not, hitting anyone, girl or boy, was not acceptable. Busting through the door, I was pretty sure I'd found who I was looking for. A plain-looking brown-haired girl lay on the bed, glasses askew, a red-haired boy was at the foot of the bed trying to pull down her jeans. There was a red welt on her cheek where he'd struck her.

"Well, well, well," I drawled, "what do we have here?"

"Get out!" The boy's voice broke, and he flushed, dropping Becky's legs.

"You have her permission to take her clothes off?" I quirked a brow at the comatose girl.

"Of course. She's my girlfriend," he sputtered, the flush staining his cheeks darker.

"Just because she's your girlfriend doesn't automatically give you permission to do anything you want to her body. Especially when she's unconscious."

"It's got nothing to do with you. Get out." He raised an arm and pointed at the door behind me. I ignored him.

"Interesting thing just happened downstairs," I said conversationally. "A young man had drugged a girl with the intent to have sex with her while she was out cold."

"W-w-what?" he squeaked.

"That's called rape," I offered up. "Just because she doesn't say no, doesn't mean yes. And being unconscious is a dead giveaway."

I looked from Becky, then back to him. "What's your name?"

"Blake Stevens," he blurted, then realized what he'd done and suddenly spun away, muttering, "Oh shit."

"It's only fair I give you the same treatment I gave to Cory Blanard, Blake Stevens." He blanched when I said Cory's name. He was busted, and he knew it. He suddenly made a run for the door, but I grabbed his wrist as he drew level with me and jolted him with electricity. Just like Cory, he fell to the floor, seizing. And just like Cory, he lost control of his bladder. Kids. No control.

Stepping over him, I crossed to the bed, tugged Becky's jeans back up, and tossed her over my shoulder. No one stopped me when I carried her through the house and out to my car—it had me shaking my head at the youth of today. Did no one look out for their friends anymore? Technically, I was abducting two teenage girls, and they sat back and watched me do it. What a fucked-up world.

After strapping Becky into the passenger seat, I drove to the hospital. I didn't know what else I could do for these girls, and god only knows what drug and what dosage the idiots had used. The police were called, and I hung around to give my statement, sitting in the emergency waiting room while parents were called, staying until the girls responded to treatment and I knew they were okay. Hours had passed, and it was almost one in the morning by the time I was done.

Walking across the hospital parking lot to my car, I froze. Was someone behind me? I'd swear I'd heard footsteps, yet when I looked over my shoulder, no one was there. When I'd arrived at the hospital, the parking lot had been packed, and I'd been forced to park a fair distance from the entrance. Now it was eerily deserted, with only a handful of cars. Not that the dark spooked me. It was just spooky in general.

With a shrug, I continued on, pulling up short when a vampire appeared in front of me. He didn't look happy. In his hands were two blades. Coupled with the fangs extending from his gums, he made a formidable opponent.

"What do you want?" Bending my knees, I braced myself, hands at my sides, a flaming dagger in each.

"Your blood, for starters, bitch." He snarled, lunging. I dodged, swiping with my own blade. We both missed, regrouped, and circled each other.

"That's kinda random, douche. You hang out at hospitals a lot, waiting for your next victim?"

"You killed my friend. I'm gonna make you pay." *Oh shit.* What I'd suspected with Nate had now come true. One of the vamps I'd offed did have friends who gave a damn that they were dead. My bad.

"Maybe you wanna join him?" I taunted, wriggling my blades at him.

"Bitch." He lunged again, and around and around we went. I'd slashed him over a dozen times, he'd missed me, and I wondered if he'd ever done this before because he was terrible at it. He looked dark and mean and threatening, but he didn't have the goods to follow through. That made me laugh, and a snort escaped, enraging him. He came at me, and I roundhouse kicked him, knocking a blade from his hand and sending it clattering across the asphalt. Switching out a dagger for my flaming lasso, I did a quick check over my shoulder to make sure we were alone in the parking lot—it wouldn't do to have a civilian catch me waving fire around.

That was my mistake, of course. Taking my eyes off him, even for a split second. I roared in pain as his blade buried deep in my shoulder. I lost my connection with the lasso, but I still had my other blade, and I swung it around and into the side of his neck. We fell, and he landed on top of me, crushing the air from my lungs. The pain in my shoulder was excruciating. The blade was still in place, his hand still wrapped around the hilt, and the jarring impact pushed it in further.

His eyes were green with a hint of red at the edges, and they stared into mine as I twisted the knife in his neck. This wouldn't kill him, but it would hurt like fuck and incapacitate him for a few seconds. Enough to whip the blade out, reposition my arm between us, and slide the knife deep into his chest. He froze, then poof. I was lying on the ground, covered in blood and ash.

"Gross." I coughed, spitting out vampire ash. I'd never killed one on top of me before, and I made a mental note not to do so again because they landed all over you. The cough jarred the dagger still buried in my shoulder, and screwing my face up, I grabbed the handle and pulled. "Faaaarrrrkkkk." I hissed, almost passing out from the pain. Son of a bitch, this sucked big time. Cradling my arm to my chest, I struggled into a sitting position. I had to get out of here before someone came out of the hospital and spotted me. Dragging myself to my feet, I leaned against my car, contemplating my next step, when my phone vibrated.

Pulling it out of my back pocket, I looked at the screen. Nate. How the hell did he have my number? And how the hell was his number in my phone? I didn't see him program it in. With a sigh, I swiped.

"Yeah?" I answered, doing my best to sound bright and bubbly and hide the pain throbbing through my shoulder and down my arm.

"Where are you?" Nate demanded.

"At the hospital."

Silence, then, "You're hurt?" Was that concern in his voice?

I laughed, a harsh, pain-filled sound. "Would a fire demon come to the hospital if she was injured?" I bit out, "No. I had some business to attend to. I'm all done now. Just leaving."

"What's wrong?"

"Nothing. Why?"

"Something is wrong. I can hear it in your voice. Don't lie to me, Paige."

I was silent again, wondering how much to tell him, when a car turned into the parking lot. I dropped down to hide, unable to stop the groan at the sudden movement.

"You're hurt." Damn him and his super vampy skills. I had this under control. I knew I could heal myself. Rae and I had discovered it in Grandpa's fire slinger book. I needed to flame. To allow myself to be consumed entirely by my fire. Only I couldn't do that in the parking lot of the hospital. I couldn't do it in my apartment either. I'd burn the entire building down. I needed somewhere totally private, somewhere where there was no risk of being seen. Somewhere perfect for a fire demon. Grandma's house. Technically, Rae's house now, but to me, it would always be Grandma's house.

"Paige, you still with me?" Nate's voice through the phone jerked me out of my thoughts.

"Yeah, yeah, I'm good. Look, I've just got one more thing to take care of, okay? Sorry, I know you said we had to work tonight, and I'm not reneging. It's just... something came up that I had to deal with."

"Something that involved you taking humans to a hospital."

"Just give me an hour or so, and I'm all yours."

"I look forward to that."

I opened my mouth to retort to his innuendo, but he'd hung up. Peeking through the windows of my car, I searched for the vehicle that had just arrived, saw it had parked near the entrance. A man and a heavily pregnant woman were slowly making their way inside. Once they were out of sight, I stood and made my way around to the driver's side, sliding inside with gritted teeth. Now I knew what being stabbed felt like, and I had to say, not a fan.

Driving one-handed was a challenge, but the roads were clear at this hour of the morning. Glancing at the clock on the dash, I calculated I had enough time to get to Grandma's, flame, then get back to my apartment with minutes to spare. I pictured Nate in my mind, waiting with arms folded across his chest, leaning with feigned patience against my apartment door, and smirked. I guessed someone as powerful as him wasn't used to being kept waiting. Too bad.

Of course, I could have told him I was injured. He could have healed me without all of this drama, but I'd also figured out something else while I was searching for the girls at the party. My hearing isn't that good. Usually. Only ever since Nate had healed me with his blood? My senses were heightened. My vision was clearer than ever before, my sense of smell intensified, my hearing vastly improved. That was why I'd overheard the boys in the bakery. And that was how I'd found them at the party. Nate's blood had changed me. I didn't know if it was a permanent thing, but I did know I didn't want any more of it. Although the devil on my shoulder pointed out how cool these enhancements were, two girls would be waking up tomorrow morning violated if it weren't for them.

"Damn it!" I slammed my fist against the steering wheel in frustration. Damned if you do, damned if you don't. Activating the Bluetooth on my phone, I called Rae.

"Paige? It's almost two in the morning. Is everything okay?"

"Shit, sorry. I forgot about the time." Where was my head? I was using hands-free via the car speakers, and Rae sounded like she was all around me. It was disconcerting, to say the least.

"You can call me day or night, hun, no matter what. But since you're calling in the early hours of the morning, something must be wrong. Spill."

"How does this flame thing work?"

"Are you hurt?" she shot back. I shrugged, then winced at the reminder—do not move your shoulder, idiot.

"Just a scratch, but I'd like to try the flaming thing, negate the healing period."

"And how did you get scratched?" she drawled, knowing I was lying.

"A really big cat?" I joked. I didn't want to tell Rae what I'd been doing since she'd left. She was SIA now, and they frowned at rogue vigilantes like me. I had to trust that Nate wasn't going to turn me in. I didn't think Rae would if she knew, but I couldn't put her in that position. What she didn't know couldn't get her into trouble.

"Right," she scoffed. "Don't tell me then. Your funeral." Rae had never been the type to push and pry, and right now, I couldn't have loved her more. "So, the flaming thing is pretty easy. Just call your fire to you and picture it in your mind, like a giant fire bubble, and you're in the middle. The first time I did it, I panicked and didn't know how to extinguish the flame once I was healed. Jordan ended up dousing me with the hose, but I've done it a few times now with no problems."

"No special words or incantations or anything?"

"Nope. Just like everything else with your flame. Think about it, and it will happen. Just be somewhere safe. Somewhere non-flammable. And do it nude if you don't want your clothes to turn to ash!"

"Got it. Thanks, Rae."

"You going to Grandma's house?" No wonder the SIA wanted her. She was a step ahead of me.

"Yeah. Now I know why Grandpa decided to build way out here."

"It has its appeal, that's for sure. Let me know how it goes, okay?"

"Sure." Disconnecting the call, I slowed and turned into the long driveway leading to Grandma's house. It was pitch black out here, with no streetlights, and the place was in total darkness. Again, utterly eerie, but something I was used to. As kids, we spent many sleepovers in the big old house.

Letting myself in, I flicked on the hallway light. The hallway ran the length of the house, from the front door to back, and I hurried down the hall now.

The back lawn was a scorched mess thanks to my siblings and cousins all practicing our fire demon skills—it was the perfect location to heal myself. Flicking on the outdoor light, I opened the back door and stood on the deck. There was barely a breeze, and the night sounds were loud in the silence.

I blew out a breath, crossed to the first step, and sat down. I untied my Nikes and slid my feet out, whipping off my socks and stuffing them into the shoes. Next was my jeans, tricky to unbutton one-handed, but if I didn't want my clothes to go up in flames, I had to take them off first. I tossed them onto the deck next to my shoes, panties followed. Now was the hard part. This was going to hurt. Sucking in a breath, I whipped my T-shirt over my head as quickly as I could, unable to contain the yell as pain surged through my entire body.

"It'll be worth it," I whispered to myself, rocking and waiting for the pain to subside to manageable levels. I glanced at the bloodstained T-shirt with a hole in it, now totally ruined. "I fucking liked that shirt, too. Asshole." I was glad I'd killed the vampire. No regrets, except for the little niggling nugget of doubt that said Nate was going to be angry with me. But I couldn't think about that now. I'd worry about what I'd tell him once I could think clearly without the thrumming pain that was clouding my mind.

My bra turned out to be the most challenging piece of clothing to remove. I couldn't twist my arm behind my back to undo it. Instead, I slid the straps down my arms, then turned it, so the clasp was at the front. Even then, I couldn't undo it one-handed and ended up shimmying it down my body and stepping out of it. The edge of one cup was stained with blood.

Stepping down onto what barely resembled a lawn, the sharp blades of grass digging into the soles of my feet, I made my way out to the middle, to an already scorched area where the flames couldn't spread. This was it. Nerves fluttered in my belly, and I was suddenly unsure. What if I got stuck like Rae did? What if I couldn't turn back? I was here alone. There was no one to turn the garden hose on me if I got into trouble. But the oozing wound on my shoulder told me I was losing too much blood. It trailed down my body in a red blaze, and if I didn't want to die from blood loss, then I'd better man the fuck up and do this thing.

Pep talk over, I closed my eyes and summoned my flame.

It surged over me, covering my body and

consuming me whole. I bathed in the glory of my fire, felt it wash away the blood staining my skin, felt the wound in my shoulder knit together, tendons, muscles, flesh, all healing with no trace of the previous trauma. There was no pain. In fact, I felt... euphoric. I stood, body ablaze, and lifted my arms out from my sides, twirling in delight. This felt fabulous.

"Impressive."

I stopped twirling and turned to face the vampire standing on the back porch.

"Don't even think about it," he warned. "You might be able to burn me, but it won't kill me—you'd best be prepared to face the consequences if you do."

His words stung because I hadn't been thinking about burning him at all. That he trusted me so little was a blow, but then who could blame him? I'd given him no reason to trust me other than my word, and even that was tenuous.

When I didn't respond, he said, "Do you need a hand extinguishing yourself? Rae mentioned you might need help."

Ah. That's why he was here. I'd called Rae. She had probably called him, for that was where her loyalties lay now. With the SIA.

"I've got it." I called my flame back, and with a whoosh, I was no longer on fire. Instead, I stood naked in the moonlight, all pain gone. No more blood, no more wound. Two seconds later, I remembered I was stark naked and quickly spun, presenting my back to Nate, my cheeks heating. He cleared his throat, but I refused to look at him.

"Inside. Now." His voice told me he was in no mood for an argument. I hesitated a second too long, it seemed, because hard fingers curled around my upper arm, and I was propelled into the house. He had no problems crossing the threshold, and I frowned. How could he come inside? He hadn't been invited.

"Hey!" I protested, wriggling out of his grip.

"Get dressed, then meet me in the den." His voice was clipped, and I figured he was angry. He'd obviously worked out I'd killed another vampire, and he was as pissed as hell about it.

"My clothes are out on the deck, dick." Urgh, why couldn't I control my mouth? He was already angry with me; did I have to make it worse?

"Wear something of Rae's."

"You've met her, right? She's an Amazon compared to me. Nothing of hers would fit." Why oh why was I arguing with him, wearing nothing but my skin? *Shut your mouth, Paige, and just do what he asks!*

A whisper of air blew my hair from my face, then he was back, my clothes being pushed against my chest. I automatically took them. "Thanks." But he was gone—waiting in the den, I assumed.

Carrying the bundle of clothes upstairs, I let myself into the bedroom Rae had claimed as hers and tossed the clothes on the bed. My panties and jeans were okay, but I wasn't putting on the bloodstained bra, and my T-shirt was ruined. I rummaged in Rae's drawer and pulled out a black tank. It was too big, but it would do. Pulling it over my head, I frowned at my reflection in the mirror. The way the fabric clung to my breasts, it was apparent I wasn't wearing a bra, but I shrugged. He'd seen me, all of me, more than once.

Pulling on my panties and jeans, I carried my Nikes in hand and made my way downstairs, barefoot. When I walked into the den, I was greeted by a glowering Nate.

"Where have you been?" he demanded, stopping mid-pace when I entered the room. Oh crap. In my determination to prevent the rape of two teenage girls, I'd ignored the fact that he'd told me we had to work tonight. Although, to be fair, he hadn't called earlier, searching for me. It had been one in the morning when he'd eventually reached out, way beyond the sunset he'd initially said. Feeling justified, I squared my shoulders and gave as good as I got.

"Excuse me? Did we have an appointment? Because you were not at my door at sunset." My voice dripped ice, and his eyes widened. He wasn't expecting to be challenged. Good.

"I told you we had work to do." Hands on hips, he towered over me, doing his best to intimidate. It was working, but damned if I'd let him see it.

"Yes. You did. You didn't show up at sunset. Obviously, I had things to do of my own. I am not at your beck and call." Turning my back on him, I held my breath as I made my way into the kitchen, burying my face in the fridge to hide my slight feeling of terror at standing up to him. My hand only shook a little as I pulled out a bottle of wine. God knows I could use the hit of alcohol. I made a mental note to replace Rae's stock.

"Where were you?" Not so aggressive, more curious than anything. I held up the bottle, and he nodded, so I grabbed two glasses and fiddled with the cork, my fingers not cooperating.

"You're not dressed for hunting."

I could practically feel the heat of his gaze and swallowed. I'd forgotten in the few brief hours I'd been away from him just what a devastating effect his presence had on me.

"No. I wasn't hunting." I relented somewhat, remembering that I had made a deal with him. I could make this easy on myself, or I could antagonize him every step of the way—and pay the consequences.

"Who were you with? A man?" Was that a hint of jealousy? Surely not.

"None of your business if I was," I retorted, feeling a blush heat my cheeks. Jesus, I wasn't a prude, not by any means, but talking about sex with this man was not on my list of things to do. Especially when I'd been fantasizing about fucking his brains out.

"Must've been a hell of a date if he left you bleeding." Nate's eyes traveled to my now-healed shoulder, then back to meet my angry gaze.

"None. Of. Your. Business," I ground out.

"You know, if I were to take you on a date, I'd leave you aching in another way entirely," he drawled, his innuendo clear.

"What are you doing?" I whispered, horrified, intrigued, and impossibly turned on.

"Playing with fire, it seems."

"Too bad," I grumbled, my cheeks flushing again, "because we are not discussing this."

"Spitfire—"

"Bite me," I snapped, shoving the bottle at him. "Open this."

I flopped onto the sofa in the den, beyond agitated. Nate followed, a glass of wine in each hand, handing one to me before lowering himself onto the couch by my side.

"Let's start over," Nate suggested. I sipped my wine and looked at him over the rim of the glass, waiting for him to elaborate.

"I came to your apartment earlier. You didn't answer. You weren't there."

"You let yourself in?" Why wasn't I surprised? The invasion of privacy niggled.

"No." He shook his head. "I listened. For your heartbeat. You weren't there."

"Oh. And we had work to do." Now I felt terrible.

I'd sworn to help him. Instead, I'd let him down. "So we lost another night. Sorry."

"When you didn't answer... I thought you'd run." My head snapped up, catching the storm gathering in his eyes.

"I promised I wouldn't," I muttered.

"You tried before," he pointed out.

Blowing out an exasperated breath, I played with my braid. "Look. You said it yourself. I am going to have to trust you, and you are going to have to trust me. If you can't do that, you may as well take me in now."

My heart was thundering in my chest, and I hoped he wouldn't call my bluff. He watched me from the sofa, then breathed in through his nose as if drawing in my scent.

"You're scared." It wasn't a question.

Rather than admit any such thing, I blurted out the first thing that came into my head. "Coffee?"

Nate raised his half-full glass of wine. Oh. Right. Again, my cheeks heated, and I hated the telltale blush, knowing he saw every little detail.

"The question is," he continued, "why are you scared? Scared of what? Me? I promise you, Spitfire, when you're on my team, working with me rather than against me, I will protect you with everything I have. I will allow no harm to come to you." His words were comforting, but that wasn't what had my breath hitching in my throat and my heart pounding. The truth was, I was scared of my attraction to him. I was scared that I couldn't keep my hands to myself. And I was terrified of the consequences if I succumbed to the urges I was barely keeping under control because I was one hundred percent sure if I instigated anything with him, he would take what I had to offer and more.

Changing the subject, I told him what I'd overheard that afternoon and where I'd been all evening. He listened in total silence, not interrupting once. Finally, my words ran out, and I waited for his response.

"Cory Blanard and Blake Stevens, you say?"

"Why? What are you going to do?" I was suddenly worried about the boys. I mean, I shouldn't be. They were assholes for what they had been planning to do, but I'd dealt with them. It was over. Plus, the police were now involved. The girls' blood would be tested; charges would be laid.

"What needs to be done," he growled, rising to his feet and setting his empty glass down on the coffee table. I jumped to my feet, too, tiny against his big frame.

"Don't you hurt them!" I protested, grabbing hold of his wrist as if I could stop him.

"They don't deserve your protection."

"I know they don't. But they're kids. They deserve a second chance." I couldn't face the thought that he was going to go out and kill those boys.

"They hurt you. Turnaround is fair play."

He thought I'd been injured by the boys. And now I had to admit my latest indiscretion, the one I'd been hoping to keep on the down low because, besides being afraid of my attraction to him, I was also painfully aware that I didn't want to disappoint him. It rankled like a splinter under my skin.

"It wasn't them," I admitted, turning my back.

"Who then?"

Spinning back to face him, I put on my brave face and told him everything. "I was jumped by a vampire when I was leaving the hospital. We... got into it... and he managed to get past my defenses when I was distracted."

"Distracted by what?"

"Checking that no one could see us, that no one was around."

"Jesus Christ. Why didn't you call me?" He ran a hand through his hair, and I wanted to smooth the tousled strands.

"Oh right, I should have totally said, excuse me one second before you tear my throat out. I just have to call a friend. *He jumped me.*" I was agitated now, unable to read his reaction. I'd been expecting him to be angry with me, but he seemed almost... indifferent. I didn't know what to think, and it made me defensive. Snatching up my glass, I headed back to the kitchen, poured more wine, gulped it down.

"Take it easy on that stuff," Nate said from behind me.

"Ha!" I scoffed. "Being half fire demon has given me a strong constitution. And you're not the boss of me," I added, once more defiant.

I heard him sigh, then the click of the door closing. What the hell? He'd just...left? No goodbye? How rude. I gulped down another glass of wine, enjoying the buzz, but I was almost out; only a few drops remained in the bottom of the bottle. Regardless, I tipped it into my glass. No use wasting it. I'd buy Rae another bottle. Hell, I'd buy her a dozen.

The oblivion I'd been hoping to find in alcohol wouldn't be tonight, which meant I had to deal with my emotions, which were always on the surface whenever Nate was around. Placing my glass a little too heavily in the sink, I winced when the stem broke, and my hand impaled itself on the broken glass.

"Fuck."

"I can't leave you for five minutes without you getting into some sort of trouble."

I jumped, not hearing him come back in. A shiver danced over me when he cradled my hand gently between his and began picking the glass out of my wound. I saw him draw a deep breath, no doubt scenting my blood. When he glanced at me, his eyes were darker than ever, hungry, and I swallowed.

"Trust me," he whispered. And god help me, I had an uncontrollable urge to do just that. I watched with wide eyes when he scored his tongue on a fang and then ran that tongue along the cut in my palm. I felt the edges of the wound pull together, healing. Then he licked again, cleaning up the remaining blood—his reward for a job well done, I suppose. I watched, dazed and unbelievably turned on.

"Your blood..." I whispered, my body leaning toward him of its own accord.

"What about it?" His voice was equally low, yet he didn't move toward me as I was him.

"It does things. To me."

"Yes." He nodded as if he were talking to a child. "It heals."

"Other things. Like my sense of smell." I breathed in deeply through my nose, got a face full of his scent. He was chocolate and musk and the outdoors and sex. I almost groaned. I knew that scent was now burned into my brain—I could identify him by smell alone from this point on. "And my hearing. I can hear a mouse fart."

He chuckled. "Yeah, vampire blood will do that. While it heals, it enhances your senses. It'll wear off within twenty-four hours."

"Oh." I was relieved and disappointed and then incredibly confused about both of those things. My mind spun. When I didn't say anything more, he released my hand and handed me a bottle in a paper bag.

"This might work better."

"What?" Opening the bag, I withdrew a bottle of whiskey and barked out a laugh. He'd gone out to get me a bottle of whiskey.

"You weren't gone long enough to go to the store."

"It was in my car. I'd bought it earlier when I realized you were going to drive me to drink."

"You confuse me," I whispered, not knowing how to react. Why couldn't he be an asshole? A total dick. Then I could hate him, and all of this would be so much easier.

"That doesn't surprise me." Reaching up, he grabbed two glasses off the shelf and took the whiskey from me, pouring a generous shot into each glass. He handed one to me, then clinked his glass against mine. "Bottoms up."

"Cheers," I responded automatically, taking a mouthful, feeling the burn down my throat; so much more potent than wine, although I liked the bubbly fruitiness of the wine.

"Can I ask you something?" he said, watching me.

"You just did." I shrugged.

"Can I ask why all the designer clothes? From your apartment, I can see you're not rolling in money. Yet, you dress exceptionally well in brand-name clothes, shoes, accessories. You don't need all that expensive drapery to look beautiful. You'd look stunning in a burlap sack."

I ignored his compliment. Ignored the way my

body straightened in response, the tingling, the heat in my abdomen. It was turning into my go-to reaction whenever he was near, and I wondered if I'd ever get used to it.

"I buy designer clothes because I like them." I shrugged. It was the truth. Mom had always thought I'd be a fashion designer; apparently, I'd had a keen interest in the fashion industry since I was a child—but it was a cutthroat business. I liked the laid-back vibe of graphic design.

"How did you get inside?" I changed the subject, feeling out of control near him, that I'd willingly give up all my secrets without a second thought.

"Rae invited me."

"She didn't need to be here?"

He ran his hand around the back of his neck and shook his head. "We've lost time tonight. It's almost dawn. You're drunk. We'll wait out the day here and start again at sundown."

He was right. The whiskey mixed with the wine was making my head spin, and I smothered a yawn. It had been another long night, and I was exhausted. Taking my glass from me, Nate set it on the sink.

"Get some rest. Tomorrow we have work to do. We're going hunting."

I didn't argue. I was too drunk to drive, and sleep sounded like a beautiful option. Upstairs, I made up two rooms, drawing the heavy drapes across the windows to block out the sun. Already the sky was changing. Dawn was chasing away the night with streaks of pink and purple.

"Which room would you prefer?" I asked. He was waiting in the hallway, and I crossed to stand in the doorway, ready to leave should he choose this room.

"Either." He shrugged.

"Well, I'll take this one then. I like yellow." Grandma had a color scheme in her house. All the upstairs bedrooms were decorated with a different pastel color theme.

"Goodnight, Paige."

I don't know what made me say it, but I suddenly blurted, "Stay," and gripped the front of his shirt.

"What?" He looked genuinely surprised, and my heart plummeted to my toes. *Idiot. What are you doing?*

"Sorry. No. You're right. Go. Jesus, just fucking go." My face was hot with embarrassment. *This is what you get for mixing your drinks, young lady.* I was not a whiskey drinker, let alone straight whiskey after a bottle of wine.

Releasing his shirt, I shut the door in his face and flung myself onto the bed. Hopefully, all of this will be forgotten in the morning. At least, I hoped it would.

SEVEN

I woke with a start, unsure of where I was. A heavy arm was draped across my body, and someone was pressed up close behind me.

"You're awake," Nate murmured, his voice thick with sleep. I shot out of bed so fast I tripped and sprawled across the floor, giving myself a carpet burn in the process.

"What the hell?"

"Relax." He chuckled, rolling onto his back. "Nothing happened."

"Then why are you in my bed?" I demanded, picking myself up and straightening the tank I'd borrowed from Rae.

"Uh, look around. This is my room."

And that was when I noticed the wallpaper was

a pale spring green, not lemon yellow. As was the comforter on the bed.

"What? How?" I didn't remember leaving my room, and I eyed him suspiciously. Had he brought me here?

"Hey!" he protested, sitting up. The covers fell away, revealing the smooth expanse of his naked chest. "You came in here, all forlorn and whimpering. Something about a bad dream. I asked if you wanted to stay, and you climbed right on in, curled up to me, and were out like a light."

My cheeks heated with embarrassment. I did not recall any of it. I used to sleepwalk as a child but hadn't had an episode in my adult life. What a time to start. Without a word, I hustled out of his room and returned to my own.

After a quick shower, I dressed in the same clothes as yesterday and made my way downstairs. Nate was already there, holding out a coffee.

"Thanks," I muttered, accepting it without making eye contact, instead turning my attention to the sunset out the kitchen window. I couldn't believe I'd slept the whole day! Sipping my coffee, I closed my eyes, waiting for it to caffeinate me enough to function. I opened them again to catch Nate studying me intently.

"What?" I grumbled. He laughed. Long and loud, his head thrown back, his white teeth gleaming. "Stop laughing at me!" I almost stomped my foot. Almost. He sobered somewhat, still chuckling to himself.

"For such a bright and bubbly spitfire, you sure are grumpy in the morning," was all he said, finishing his own coffee, rinsing his mug, and setting it to drain on the sink. "Drink up. We need to get going."

"Where?"

"Back to your place so you can get changed. Then we're going hunting."

"Hunting in general, or do you have someone specific in mind?" I crossed my arms over my chest and tilted my head. Memories of last night were coming back to me. Throwing myself at him, the look of surprise on his face. My cheeks burned with the memory.

"I'll tell you on the way," he replied cryptically. He commandeered my car, saying he'd return for his later. Once he was behind the wheel, he began talking. "What do you know about ghouls?"

"Absolutely nothing," I replied. It was the truth.

"As the name suggests, ghouls consume human

flesh—preferably dead—and they can take on the form of the last person they ate."

A shudder ran through me. "Gross," I muttered. Vampires drinking blood was one thing, but ghouls eating flesh? I swallowed and opened the window to let in some fresh air, my stomach heaving at the thought.

"That makes them challenging to find. Especially if they decide to take on that human's life. They can live for several years undetected."

"And how are they detected?"

"The form they've taken over doesn't age. So, after a few years, people start to get suspicious. Plus, they run out of food and move on to their next meal."

"What are you saying?" I had a vision of a ghoul's freezer full of body parts, each neatly labeled in preparation for Sunday's roast.

"Some ghouls will eat and run, meaning they won't consume the entire corpse, just enough to satisfy their appetite for the moment. Other ghouls may join in and, between them, demolish the corpse. Sometimes it's just discarded. But the smarter ones will stalk their prey, study their life, then kill them and assimilate into that life for as long as possible before moving on to the next."

"So. Ghouls kill humans?"

"Affirmative. What? Did you expect they simply dug up graves and ate the rotting flesh? Or had a deal at the local funeral parlor?"

"Urgh." I gagged at the visual.

"They like their meat dead—freshly dead is best, but they will eat a rotting corpse if they're hungry enough. They can substitute human meat with animal meat for a while, but it is human flesh that keeps them alive."

"Stop," I gasped, fearing I'd throw up. This was the grossest thing I'd ever heard. I rolled the window down further and practically stuck my whole head out, uncaring that my hair was now all over the place.

"The only way to kill a ghoul is by destroying their brain," he continued, uncaring that I was a lovely shade of green. "Either bash their head in, shoot them between the eyes, or decapitation will work too."

I closed my eyes and sucked in deep breaths until the nausea passed. I'd been killing vampires; I could kill a ghoul, too. If I had to. But why did I have to?

"Why are we hunting ghouls, though? I mean, why do you need me?"

"Because ghouls can sense when a vampire is nearby. He will sense me a mile away. I need the element of surprise, and that's where you come in."

"And there are ghouls in Maxxan?" I'd had no idea, although a couple of the vampires I'd interrogated had alluded to the fact that trouble was brewing in my town.

"Yes." He didn't sugarcoat any of it. Despite the fact the very thought of getting up close and personal with a flesh-eating ghoul made me want to hurl, I did what I always did in such situations. I asked myself, what would Rae do? She'd get the job done, was the answer. She'd push down any fear and squeamishness, buckle up, and do what was necessary. I'd agreed to help Nate, and that's what I'd do.

Mentally squaring my shoulders, I listened as he outlined his plan. Stake out the nightclub, Enchant. Nate showed me a photo of the ghoul we were looking for, a rather attractive blonde man with blue eyes and a wicked smile. He had a British accent, which would make it even easier to pick him from the crowd.

Arriving back at my apartment, Nate insisted I shower to remove any traces of his scent. Then I was to dress as I usually did for hunting, like a girl on the prowl. Appeared vamps and ghouls alike went for the scantily clad women. Nate said something about retrieving his car and disappeared.

Within forty minutes, I was ready, a skin-tight red dress that plunged almost to my navel, black thigh-high boots, hair piled high on my head to expose my neck, and heavy makeup. In outfits like this, I didn't feel like myself. It wasn't really me; it was my persona, and I secretly loved it, loved that no one knew the real girl behind the body and makeup, behind the external packaging. Of course, the creatures I met when dressed like this weren't interested in getting to know the girl. They either wanted to fuck or drink my blood, or both. And so far, I'd avoided all of those scenarios—I guess it was only a matter of time before my luck ran out.

Nate was back and waiting. He looked me up and down, nodded, and opened the door, waiting for me to pass through ahead of him.

"This way." He moved to place a hand at the small of my back, then just as quickly pulled away. I frowned, not liking the twinge of hurt at his reluctance to touch me.

"Don't want my scent on you," he explained, as if sensing my sudden disquiet. I didn't answer;

instead, my mind was a whirl—why was I disappointed he hadn't put his hand on me?

"You're very quiet." He spoke softly just above my ear, and I ignored the weird sensation that swirled through my belly.

"Just thinking." I shrugged.

"About?"

"Everything. You. Me. My situation."

He stopped. His expression became guarded. "You're not thinking of running again, are you?"

"What?" Far from it. "No." Hadn't we already covered this? If he thought I was going to run every five minutes, then this would be impossible.

"I said I'd help, and I will. I promise." I exaggerated the word, trying to drill it into his thick skull that I'd made my decision, and I'd stand by it. And him. "Trust me. I know you don't, but you should. I'm trusting you tonight. You could be hanging me out to dry for all I know. I'm letting you use me as ghoul bait, for Christ's sake. I don't know anything about ghouls, how strong they are, what their weaknesses are. How easily one would be able to incapacitate me. Eat me." I shuddered at the imagery.

He paused before answering, seeming to choose his words. "I will be there. Watching. You won't see me, but I will be there, and I won't allow any harm to come to you."

"Nate..." I paused, unsure of how to proceed. "All my life, I've been taught that vampires are... bad...evil. You haven't given me much of an adjustment period, but I'm trying. I wouldn't be here now if that weren't the case. But what if it turns out I'm wrong? If it turns out you are a—" I was going to say monster, but he cut me off before I could finish.

"Your trust in me is not misplaced." It was turning into quite a sentimental moment, which he ruined by continuing with, "There's something about me that you need to remember, Paige. I'm a hundred-and-eighty-year-old vampire. I was a soldier when I was turned. Since then, I've been a marine, a navy seal, special ops—which is why I'm now the Director of the SIA. I do what needs to be done. Understood?"

I gulped. He was serious. Deadly serious. It was no longer my own neck on the line, and I fully believed that my family would pay the price if I did run or try to harm or kill him. "Understood," I whispered, shaken. None of the research I'd done on him had revealed his extensive military background. I cursed myself for being so shallow as to think there wasn't more to this man than what I'd read on the internet.

"Good." We began walking again. I curled my hands into fists to hide the ripple of blue electricity.

We stopped at my car, and I opened the door. "You're not coming?"

He shook his head. "I'll follow, don't worry."

Right. "And you think I can draw him out? Because I'm wearing revealing clothes?"

"This will work because you're young and vibrant and are exuding a delicious energy that will attract him. You're just his type."

"Yuk," I grumbled, sliding my key into the ignition and starting the car. Then I had a thought.

"What about zombies?" I asked, before closing the door.

"What about them?"

"Are they real?"

"What do you think?"

"No, I don't think they're real. I mean, how could they be? We already have ghouls, which sounds like the same sort of thing."

"Zombies eat brains, not flesh," he pointed out.

"So, they're real?"

"Sorry, that's classified," he replied drolly.

"You could have said that to begin with instead

of being a dick about it," I grumbled, slamming the door. Then another thought hit me, and I wound down the window. "Ghouls don't eat fire demons, do they?"

"I have no idea. Lure him in, and take him to the warehouse. Treat him just as you would a vampire, and you'll be fine. I won't be far away." And then he was gone. I hadn't seen him move, but suddenly I was alone. Straightening my shoulders, I breathed in a deep breath and got into character. I could do this. One British ghoul coming right up.

EIGHT

"'Ello luv, what's a pretty little thing like you doing in a place like this?" The unmistakable British accent had me swiveling on my bar stool in surprise. I'd had no sense of a supernatural entity nearby. It was busy tonight, but mostly with human activity. I'd sensed no vampires at all, and I wondered if it was due to the ghoul being in town. Were vampires afraid of ghouls?

"Oh, you know,"—I plastered a smile on my face and fluttered my fake eyelashes at the disturbingly handsome man who slid onto the stool next to mine —"looking for some fun."

Ian Blackwell was drop-dead gorgeous. His hair was whiter than blonde, and his blue eyes were mesmerizing. No wonder he wanted to stay in his own skin—it was divine. He was as tall as Nate, but not as broad. His body had a lean edge to it, and I wondered briefly if he was hungry. I blanched at the thought, then cursed myself for such thoughts, for he leaned toward me, concern on his face. "Everything all right, luv? You look a little peaky."

"Sorry." I pushed down all thoughts of the flesh-eating ghouls and smiled again. "I'm fine, it's just...."

"What is it, luv? You can tell me." He leaned in closer, his knee pressing against mine, his hand landing on my thigh and squeezing ever so softly. Testing my suitability as a snack?

"It's my boyfriend." I sighed, turning sad eyes to him. "Ex-boyfriend, I should say. He dumped me yesterday." I blinked rapidly, as if dispelling tears. "And yet I just saw him...here...with another girl." I lowered my face, letting loose tendrils of hair swing forward.

"Oh, sweetheart." Bingo, he fell for it hook, line and sinker. His arm was now around my shoulders, and our bodies pressed close together. "He's not worth the air you breathe, I promise ya. How about you let me buy you another drink, and I can cheer you up?"

"That would be wonderful." I smiled and turned

my face up to his, losing myself in the sparkling sapphires of his eyes.

My glass was never empty, and I could feel the alcohol taking effect. This ghoul was doing an excellent job of getting me drunk. He was also getting handsy. He'd run his palm up and down my thigh for a while, and when I didn't protest or move away, he turned his attention on other body parts, mostly my neck. It was weird. I would have thought a vampire would have been obsessed with my neck, but it appeared Ian was a neck guy, for he kept running his fingers up and down my throat, then curling them around the nape of my neck. When he cupped my chin and ran his thumb across my bottom lip, my control slipped, and I shuddered in revulsion.

Mistaking my shudder for desire, he leaned closer. "Shall we go somewhere a little more private, luv?" His lips touched my ear, and another shiver danced over me.

"Yes!"

He chuckled at my enthusiasm, threaded his fingers through mine, and tugged me forward, sliding me off the barstool until we stood chest to chest, hip to hip.

"I know just the place." His voice was lower,

thicker, and his eyes darker. My heart jumped in anticipation, but I was pretty sure we were anticipating different things. He wanted sex. I wanted to tie him up and torture him.

"I have a place..." I touched my tongue to my lower lip and looked up at him from beneath my lashes. I had to convince him to go to the warehouse with me—if we went back to his place, things could get tricky—like I'd burn his house down, and that would draw unwanted attention.

His free arm curled around my waist, and he hugged me harder against him. His desire for me unmistakable. I felt the color drain from my face and quickly ducked my head to hide my reaction. Sucking in a breath, I did my best to compose myself. Soon, I promised myself. Soon I'd have him in the warehouse, and then it would all be worth it. Then I could have my fun. That's if Nate didn't stop me. Nate had said he wanted to interrogate the ghoul, but surely he would let me help?

"Let's go." He led the way out of the club, dragging me behind him with hard fingers around my wrist.

"Slow down," I protested, almost falling. His grip was going to bruise, and I frowned. Something had changed. His energy had changed and when he shot me a look over his shoulder, so had his eyes. The sparkling blue of earlier was gone. Now he was as cold as steel. Had he figured me out? Had he seen through my act?

We were close to the door now, and he was clearing a path through the crowd of humans who were gyrating to the DJ's beats. I tried to catch a glimpse of Nate, but being so short, I had no chance of spotting anyone above the heads surrounding me. A twinge of unease had me pulling back, tugging against the grip he had on me. He frowned at me. "What?"

"Wow! Rude much?" When I dug my heels in, he had no option but to stop. He'd been looking around the club, his eyes scanning, but my words brought his attention back to me, and immediately his face softened, as did his grip on my wrist.

"Sorry, luv. I thought I'd caught a glimpse of someone I knew. Didn't want to get tied up chatting with him, so I forgot my manners for a minute. I do apologize."

He sounded so sincere, and if he weren't a ghoul, I would have liked him. I wondered if it was Nate he'd caught a glimpse of, but I couldn't sense any vampires nearby, and Nate had told me he'd be keeping his distance. Maybe it was someone or something else entirely that Ian had seen.

Rather than drag me along behind him, this time he tugged me to his side and slid his arm around my waist, accommodating his long stride to my much shorter one, and we made our way outside. I welcomed the night air. It had been hot and claustrophobic in the club, and even though it was warm out, it was still a welcome relief to breathe in the fresh air.

"You said you had a place?" Ian hinted.

"Yes. Where we won't be disturbed."

A red Ferrari Pista pulled up in front of us, and a man slid out from behind the wheel, tossing the keys to Ian. I couldn't help but ogle the glamorous sports car.

"I didn't know Enchant had valet service." The car was gorgeous, slick, and sexy, and I eyed it appreciatively.

"They don't." Ian opened the passenger door for me, and I obediently slid inside, glancing around to see if I could spot Nate lurking nearby. I couldn't, and that feeling of apprehension was back. He wouldn't set me up, would he? This wasn't his solution to deal with me, was it? Let a ghoul kill me, remove him from all involvement? Blue electricity sparked from my fingertips, and I curled my hands into fists. Do not set fire to this car, I scolded myself. Stay focused. It will be fine. Nate had said to take Ian to the warehouse. He was probably waiting there.

Feeling somewhat reassured, I plastered on a smile when Ian slid behind the wheel and gunned the engine.

"Where to?" he asked. I gave him directions and sat back, enjoying the ride. I appreciated the luxury of his car, the leather seats, the impressive dash. He saw me admiring and smiled. "You like?"

"Yes," I breathed, "very much." It was true. I did. But then I'd always liked the finer things in life; unfortunately, I didn't have the bank balance to own luxuries such as this one, but I appreciated it while I could. Who knew if I'd ever get to ride in a Ferrari again?

We pulled up outside the warehouse. "Interesting place," Ian commented, turning off the lights. It was pitch dark outside.

"I like it." I smiled, and before I knew it, he'd leaned over the center console, wrapped a hand around the back of my neck, and pulled me toward him, his mouth coming down hard on mine. His lips were warm—I don't know what I was expecting. Cold, lifeless flesh, perhaps? I played along as best I could. His kiss wasn't aggressive; he wasn't trying to shove his tongue down my throat, and for that, I was grateful—I'd have blown my cover if that were the case. Rather than a thrill of delight at his advance, I was plotting my next move. Get him into the warehouse.

My mind jerked back to the present when his hand squeezed my breast. I pulled away, tried to sound sultry and seductive rather than repulsed. "Let's go inside."

He smiled and released me. I quickly turned to open my door, glad to hide my expression from him. It was getting harder and harder to act like I was into him. For the briefest of moments, I longed to be an ordinary girl, to go on a date with a guy, to share a kiss, maybe more, with no intent other than to enjoy the moment. But those days were gone, I scolded myself. Maxxan was overrun with vampires and apparently ghouls, and I was a fire demon—not an ordinary girl.

Dragging in a deep breath, I stepped out of the car and squared my shoulders, game face on. I indicated the door and murmured, "After you." I had flashbacks of the last time I was here, doing this with Nate. Unlike last time, Ian stepped in ahead of me, giving me the precious seconds I needed to unleash my fire lasso. Only I didn't get to use it.

Nate was already there.

"What the hell?" Ian sputtered.

"Blackwell, long time no see." Nate's voice was as cold as ice despite the friendliness of his words.

"Wilder. Should have known. Glad I brought backup. Thought she was too good to be true." He sneered at me over his shoulder, and I bristled. Then his words sank in. Backup? Strong arms banded around me from behind, and I squealed in surprise. I hadn't been expecting more ghouls.

Nate moved with lightning speed, grabbing hold of Ian, and the two of them wrestled in a blaze of movement that I couldn't follow. Which left me to deal with the ghoul on my back. A heavy punch to my temple had me seeing stars, and I staggered, blinking. Then a blow to my stomach winded me, making breathing virtually impossible. That's when I realized it wasn't only one attacker. Through bleary eyes, I counted at least five.

Summoning a sword and dagger, I armed myself. This wasn't how I'd intended any of this to go down, but damned if I wouldn't put up one hell of a fight. Facing the five ghouls, I waited. Ian and

Nate were crashing around the warehouse, and it was up to me to deal with these five on my own.

Taking aim with my dagger, I threw the blade, which sank into the neck of the ghoul closest to me, but it kept coming. Fast. With a sword in hand, I swung for its head. My blade sailed through the sinew and flesh, cutting through bone. The head tumbled to the ground with a thud, the body following a second later. This was my first ghoul kill, and I watched as it, too, disintegrated into ash.

No time to ponder this latest revelation, as another ghoul was almost upon me. Heart pounding, I danced back and slashed at his legs, lopping the left clean off. I tried not to gag as blood poured out in a slick pool of black. The ghoul fell to his one remaining knee and grabbed for my ankle. I swung my blade hard, severing another head. Two down, three to go.

I lunged and sliced, sweat dampening my skin as I swung my sword, every strike connecting with a ghoul until there were no more. I stood panting, my sword clasped in both hands in front of me, legs bent, ready for another attack, black ooze dripping from me.

"She is something, isn't she?" Nate said to Ian, who was chained to the interrogation pole. Ian was looking at me with a stunned look on his face. Around me was nothing but ashes turning soggy in black ooze. Straightening, I released my sword and wiped my palms on my now ruined dress.

"I would have negotiated a clothing allowance if I'd known you were going to ruin all my clothes," I said to Nate.

"How did she do that?" Ian cut in before Nate could respond.

"Do what? Kill ghouls?" I asked, annoyed that he thought a woman wasn't capable of such a thing.

"Turn them to ash!" Ian replied, looking from me to Nate and back again.

Nate caught my eye and gave me a slight shake of his head, indicating to keep my mouth shut. I did, for my mind was busy digesting what Ian had said. Turning the ghouls to ash. I thought that was what they did when they were killed. I figured that since the same thing happened when I killed vampires that it must be a paranormal thing. But judging by Ian's reaction, maybe not? I filed it away to ask Nate about it later.

"Tell me about the missing girls." Nate changed the subject, turning on Ian, hands-on-hips, eyes blazing.

Ian laughed. "Don't know what you're talking about, mate."

I opened my mouth to ask Nate the same thing. What missing girls? What the hell was going on? I didn't get the chance. Nate punched Ian in the face. Hard. I heard bones crunching from where I stood.

Ian turned his head and spat out blood, still grinning. "You'll have to try harder than that, mate. You know I like it… rough."

"Spitfire, why don't you come over here and show Ian some of your… skills?"

"I'd be delighted." I couldn't keep the enthusiasm from my voice. Now we were talking. With a crack, my fire lasso appeared, and I snapped it over my head, the sound reverberating throughout the warehouse.

Ian's smile slipped, then disappeared entirely when the lasso whipped over his chained wrists. Immediately, the stench of burning flesh reached my nostrils. Ghouls smelled different from vampires. His flesh smelled…rotten, and I tried not to gag.

"Try not to kill him," Nate murmured in my ear, moving behind me.

"Can't promise anything," I replied, leaving the lasso in place and drawing a dagger from my flame.

"I don't know a ghoul's tolerances, how far I can push before—you know—kaput."

"Just try not to kill him until we get the information we need," was all Nate said. Then I heard the sound of the fold-up chair being put into position and knew he'd taken a seat to watch the proceedings, just as he'd done when I was the one chained to the pole.

Stepping forward, I slashed at Ian's shirt until I had unobstructed access to his skin. Similar to vampires, it was smooth, unblemished, ageless. Seemed a shame to ruin it, but I was beyond curious about his healing capabilities because he wasn't screaming in agony at the burning rope around his wrists.

"Tell me about the girls," I demanded, running the tip of the blade down his chest, not deep, but enough to make him bleed. The black ooze that trickled out made me want to hurl, but I swallowed the bile that rose in my throat and concentrated on the task at hand.

"There are no girls," he ground out. Not so cocky now, but still defiant. His eyes flashed their hatred.

"Wrong answer." I smiled, running my blade across his abdomen horizontally, deeper this time. The previous cut was still bleeding, so ghouls weren't fast healers. Or maybe they didn't heal at all? I wanted to turn to Nate and ask, but knew better than to turn my back on anyone being tortured. If Ian figured out he could cut off his own hands with the lasso and reach for me, he could easily kill me—hands or not. I knew this because a vampire had done that very thing. Of course, a blade through his heart had stopped his attack, but it was a lesson learned. Don't be complacent.

I continued to carve up Ian's front until he was a mass of oozing black wounds. He still hadn't given up any information, refusing to speak; instead, all we heard was his harsh breathing.

"Okay, I need to take this up a notch," I said to Nate. "How badly do you want him kept alive?"

"I'm starting to think he doesn't actually know anything," Nate replied. Now I turned slightly and looked at him out of the corner of my eye. What game was he playing now? He wouldn't have gone to all this trouble if he wasn't convinced Ian had the information he needed.

"You want me to off him, then?" I asked conversationally.

"May as well. You have the convenient talent of leaving no body to clean up afterward; otherwise, I'd do it. It would be my pleasure." Nate stood as if getting ready to leave.

"Okay then. Thanks Ian, this has been fun. And educational. You're the first ghoul I've ever met, and I've learned a lot tonight about your physiology and healing capabilities; however, well..." I indicated my blood-spattered dress. "I'm a mess, and a shower is in order, so..." I exchanged my dagger for my sword, grasped it in both hands, and drew back, lining up his neck. One clean slice would have it toppling in a second.

"WAIT!" Ian screamed, "Wait!"

I hesitated, sword aloft. "Yes?"

"I don't know anything about the girls, but I know someone who might... might know what is going on."

"I think you're lying, Ian." I smiled. "Not once have you asked, 'What girls?' indicating that you know precisely what Nate is talking about." I bluffed that I also knew what on earth he was talking about, but I had no idea what girls Nate was referencing.

"Fuck." He swore, tugging on the fire lasso. The terror in his eyes was genuine. He knew I meant to kill him. I wondered if Nate wanted him dead regardless, whether he gave us the info or not. I was running on adrenaline, and my demon was keen for the kill, eager for it, and I wasn't sure I'd be able to turn back at this late point.

"Byers. Leroy Byers." Ian panted, twisting and writhing against the pole.

"Who's he?" Nate asked.

"Who's he?" Ian laughed hysterically. "Only one of the most powerful ghouls there is."

"And where can we find Leroy Byers?" Nate asked.

"Redmeadows. He frequents a club there a lot. It's the best place to find him."

Nate was so close behind me I felt him stiffen. "What club?"

"Crimson Mist."

"Interesting." Nate touched a hand to my shoulder, and I took it as permission to end the conversation. I did, quick and fast. Ian didn't get a chance to scream or beg. His head was turning to ash before it hit the ground.

"Try not to get any of that crap on the seats." Nate waved a hand at my ruined dress that was dripping black ghoul blood.

"Fuck you," I replied, sliding into the passenger seat, not caring if I smeared the black substance everywhere.

"What's wrong with you?"

"Oh, let me see, maybe it could be that you didn't see fit to tell me that turning vampires—and ghouls—to ash when I kill them isn't the norm. Or maybe there's something more going on with a bunch of girls. You said you wanted my help. Well, I can't be of much help if I don't know what's going on!"

"You were a great help tonight." He smiled, and I wanted to punch him.

"I could have easily killed them all without giving you the opportunity to ask the questions you wanted. You say I have to trust you. Yeah, well, it's a two-way street, asshole." Crossing my arms over my chest, I seethed.

"You're hangry," he commented.

"Hangry? What the hell is that?"

"You get angry when you're hungry. You used up your reserves tonight—I admit I hadn't been expecting such a horde of ghouls to be accompanying Ian."

"But you were expecting some? See? You could have warned me!"

"If I'd warned you, you'd have given the whole thing away. It was best if you thought you only had Ian to deal with. You gave him your one hundred percent undivided attention, and that's exactly what we needed for tonight to work. Suppose he'd suspected for a second that you weren't entirely into him. In that case, he'd have either ditched you or suspected something was up, and we wouldn't have gotten him to the warehouse." Nate drove as he spoke, and moments later, we were outside my apartment.

"Go get changed, and I'll take you out to eat." I looked at him across the dimness of the car, unsure of this vampire. Was he playing a game with me? But he was right, I was hungry, and if he was buying, I'd play along. Plus, I needed to go pick up my car at some point.

Thankfully, the ghoul blood had only splattered on my dress and boots. I didn't have to wash my hair or re-do my makeup, so after a quick shower and costume change—black designer jeans, red ankle boots, and a white shoestring strap blouse decorated with red cherries—I was back downstairs and sliding into the passenger seat once more. I felt Nate's eyes roam over me but didn't meet his gaze, instead keeping my eyes glued to the windscreen. I'd decided that I was staying quiet until he'd given me the information he'd been withholding.

He pulled out, and in silence, we drove. The clock on the dash said it was just after one a.m. Funny, it felt later. Nate had been right. I'd expended a lot of energy in fighting the ghouls and torturing Ian. I was tired. I didn't argue when he turned off the highway into the parking lot of a waffle place on the outskirts of town.

The Waffle House was old but clean, the Formica tabletops were faded, but there were no rips in the vinyl booths, which was something. We were the only two customers.

"Coffee?" A waitress appeared, holding a coffee pot in one hand. She looked tired. Her blonde hair was pulled back into a tight ponytail, but frizzly tendrils escaped. She seemed to be mid-forties, a little overweight, and judging by how she moved, she either had bad knees or hips. Either way, something was hurting when she walked.

"Sure." I nodded, and she flipped the cup that was upside down on the table the right way up and filled it.

"How about you?" she asked Nate.

"Why not?" He smiled, and that was the exact moment her demeanor changed from disinterested and bored to very interested. And smitten. It seemed Nate had that effect on every woman he came across.

I watched through my lashes as the waitress flirted with him, and he flirted right back. The woman positively bounced away, promising to return with our order of pie.

"What if I didn't want pie?" I pouted, annoyed he'd ordered for me, but even more annoyed that he'd ordered exactly what I wanted. Without asking. How did he know?

"You don't want pie?" he asked.

"Yes, I want pie," I grumbled, frowning when he laughed.

Then he held up his hands in a peace gesture. "Okay, okay. I'm sorry."

"For?"

"Whatever it is you're mad about."

Sighing, I looked out the window, not seeing anything beyond the darkness of the night. True to her word, the waitress was back in record time with a serving of cherry pie for each of us. She topped up my coffee, and I absently smiled my thanks.

"Eat," he ordered, "then we'll talk." I picked up my fork, doing as instructed, almost groaning as the cherry pie exploded against my taste buds. Closing my eyes, I chewed, then swallowed, before digging in for another bite. I demolished the pie in seconds.

"See? Hungry," he commented.

"Talk," I replied, signaling the waitress for another slice. I was tempted to tell her to bring the whole damn thing, but didn't want to look like a pig.

"What do you want to know first?"

"The ash thing."

He nodded, took a bite of his pie, and looked at me thoughtfully. "The thing that we, I, have discovered about fire demons is that some of you—

not all—have unique talents besides the whole fire thing. Take Rae, for example. Her blood will kill a vampire. No other fire demon that we've come across has that ability. It's unique to her. But those vampires don't disintegrate into nothing. We have to dispose of the bodies. Yet you? You kill a vampire, and poof, they're gone, nothing but ash on the wind." His fingers mimed the action, and my mouth curled into a grin.

"But your blood doesn't kill them," he continued. "You have to do it the same as everyone else. Decapitation or a blade through the heart. I'm wondering if it's something to do with the Shelton line."

"So you want to study us? Find out what it is?" I prodded.

"Nope." He shrugged. "Just curious. We will document our discoveries as they appear, but no, we have no intentions of treating you—or Rae, or any of your family, for that matter—as lab rats."

Okay. That seemed reasonable. And he did raise a good point, one I hadn't thought of before. Rae could kill with her blood, and we'd thought it was because her fire demon had been triggered in childhood instead of adulthood, and that had somehow changed the chemistry of her blood. But what if that wasn't the case? What if that was as nature had intended all along? Her unique ability was always going to be hers, despite what had happened to her as a child.

"Any more questions? About the fire demon stuff?"

"Not yet. Tell me about the girls." Leaning forward, I rested my elbows on the table. Nate checked that the waitress wasn't in earshot and mimicked my pose, leaning toward me.

"Humans have been disappearing—unreported disappearances—mostly women. The homeless, runaways, prostitutes."

"From Maxxan?" I was surprised. I had no idea anyone had been going missing, but then I thought about what he'd just said. Unreported. People who wouldn't be missed.

He nodded. "Maxxan and Redmeadows. There was a similar case a couple of years back. Only those that had disappeared did turn up again. Dead. And they weren't homeless."

"You're worried it's started again?"

"It could be anything. The ghouls could be stockpiling. The vampires could be dabbling in human slaves. Either way, it's not good. The SIA can't turn a blind eye."

"How do ghouls normally get their... food?" I shuddered at the thought of them eating people.

"The sick. Elderly. Recently deceased. They also don't need to eat human meat all the time. Every few months, a top-up meal is enough to keep them going."

"What do they eat in the meantime?"

"Raw beef, usually."

"And the ghouls, you think they're responsible for the disappearances? Not vampires?"

"A camera caught a ghoul snatching a homeless kid in Redmeadows. That kid hasn't shown up since."

"You think they... ate him?"

"Possibly. The homeless, the unwanted, are a vulnerable target—no one would report it if they did go missing. The previous case we had in Redmeadows was a little different. For one, it wasn't the homeless. They were random attacks in public places. And those who were taken were reported missing. The only thing we had that could tie them together was that all the victims had visited my nightclub, Crimson Mist. What we discovered, then, was that they were being experimented on. Someone was injecting them with a cocktail of venom from vampires and werewolves combined and trying to create a super paranormal species. Only they failed."

"Jesus." I sat back against the booth and looked at him incredulously. I couldn't imagine such a thing, yet here he was, discussing it as casually as if asking if I took sugar in my coffee.

"You think it's started up again? And this Leroy Byers is involved?"

"We don't know anything. No bodies have turned up. It could be totally unrelated. As for Byers, he could be calling the shots or knows the ghoul who is. I'm after any ghoul who can give me information. We got a tip-off about Ian Blackwell being in Maxxan. I've met Ian before, hence why he'd be able to sense me if I tried to apprehend him myself."

"What next?" I sat back when the waitress reappeared with more pie. Nate waited until she left before continuing.

"I planted a tracker on the car Ian had been driving. Did you notice when we left the warehouse that it was gone?"

Shit. I hadn't. "But how? I killed the ghouls inside, and you had Ian restrained."

"Another ghoul had hung back. I assume to keep

a lookout. He'd have heard what went down in the warehouse and bolted, taking Ian's car."

"Do you think he's gone to warn Leroy Byers?"

"A phone call would do it. I suspect he's gone into hiding." Nate finished his pie and sat back, regarding me. I didn't like the way he was looking at me with a strange expression on his face. "What?"

"I need to eat."

I looked from his empty plate and back to his face, confused. "You just ate," I pointed out. "Order something else if you're still hungry."

"What I'm hungry for isn't on the menu."

"Oh!" Blood. He needed blood. I quickly crossed my arms over my chest and sat back, as far out of reach as I could get within the confines of the booth. "Don't look at me. You're not getting any of this."

He chuckled, tossed his napkin on the table, and slid out. "The waitress it is." And he was gone, moving at lightning speed.

I waited a minute, then two, before curiosity got the better of me, and I stood, making my way to the counter. No sign of the waitress. Or Nate. I could hear the late-night cook banging around in the kitchen. Silently, I made my way to the end of the counter and peeked into the storeroom at the end. Nate stood with the waitress pressed against his body, her back to his chest. One arm was around her waist, pinning her against him; the other was pressing her forehead back into his shoulder, arching her throat.

As if knowing I was looking, he raised his head. His fangs glinted with drops of her blood. From here, his eyes looked black, and something was swirling within their depths, something that told me he may have been drinking from her, but he was thinking about me. A wave of something hit me... desire? Lust? Whatever it was, it was powerful, and my body answered the call, swaying forward even as he lowered his head again, keeping his eyes locked on mine as he slowly, sensually sunk his fangs into her neck. The waitress groaned and arched against him as if in bliss, which puzzled me. He'd bitten me before. It hadn't been a fun experience; it had hurt like a bitch—which begged the question, why was this woman enjoying his bite?

Turning away, I headed back to our booth, suddenly uncomfortable. Why did it bother me watching him feed from another woman? Was it the sensuality of it? Or the way his eyes held mine, telling me that he may have been biting her, but he was thinking about me. I wriggled uncomfortably.

"It bothers you?" Nate was by my shoulder, startling me with his speed and silence.

"No," I lied, not looking at him.

"I take what I need, heal the wound, and send them on the way, none the wiser that I've had a sip from their vein."

"She won't remember?"

"Nope. A little mind compulsion, and she'll be tired, but other than that, no ill effects. And the little blood I used to heal the puncture wounds will go a long way in relieving the arthritis in her knees."

"Oh." None of this was what I'd imagined, what Dad and my uncles had drummed into us growing up. Their motto was, "All vampires are evil; they will bite you and drink your blood until you're dead." But this sexy-as-sin vampire by my side was blowing all of those preconceived notions into smithereens, and I wasn't sure what to believe anymore.

"Come on, I'll drop you back to your car." Leading the way, he called out goodnight to the waitress, then held the door open for me.

"What will you be doing?"

"Monitoring Ian's car, see where it ends up. See if any other ghouls turn up. I'll let you know when I need you again."

I was off the hook for now, so why did I feel a pang of disappointment? I should have been doing cartwheels to be free of him, but instead? Instead, I felt...disappointed. Shaking off my strange mood, I settled into the passenger seat once more and pondered the disaster my life had become.

A shrill whistle followed by, "Hey! Paige!" had me swiveling on my heel and peering down the sidewalk for whoever had summoned me. I pinpointed a curly blonde head through the crowd of people, cut off denim shorts, and a white tank. Lani, my best friend. I started to walk toward her with a smile, laughing when she wrapped her arms around me and squeezed tight.

Lani and I had been friends since our first day at grade school, and while we weren't quite as inseparable as we once were, we'd discovered our friendship outlasted the absences, that no matter how long it had been since we'd caught up, it was as if no time had passed at all.

"God, it's good to see you!" I returned her hug with genuine pleasure. The last few days had been silent from Nate, and I felt like I was on tenterhooks, waiting for something to happen. I'd thrown myself into work but was lacking the focus I usually had. Lani was just the distraction I needed.

"You too, hun." Releasing me, she stepped back and looked me up and down. "Still into the fancy duds, I see," she teased.

"Still flaunting the eighties cowboy look, I see," I shot back. Lani always had been and always would be a tomboy. Her boots, shorts, and tank were her usual attire. We were polar opposites, and maybe that was why, together, we just worked.

Linking arms, we continued down the sidewalk.

"What's new? Heard about your uncle getting himself on the wrong side of the law. That's too bad. The rumor mill said something about drugs?" The SIA had told the local police a modified version of the story, one suitable for public consumption.

"Yeah, growing marijuana. Can you believe it?"

"Honestly? No."

"Neither can we. None of us had any idea."

"I'm really sorry, Paige. That totally sucks." She gave my arm a squeeze, and I appreciated her support. Lots of old acquaintances had come out of the woodwork when news of Uncle Frank's arrest had been made public—but they only wanted the gossip, and I'd quickly shut that down. Lani had sent a simple text saying she was there for me. I loved her for it.

"Got time for a coffee?" I asked. We'd reached the bakery, and I stopped to look through the window. There were a couple of customers seated inside and plenty of spare tables.

"Sure. And a doughnut." She grinned and bounced in ahead of me. Lani was a bouncy, bubbly, loveable tomboy.

We ordered, then grabbed a table over by the window. "What's new with you?" I asked, wanting to avoid any more talk of my family.

"Oh! I've been dating the Hastings' boy." She bounced up and down in her seat, and I shook my head at her excitement. You would have thought she was eighteen by her demeanor, not twenty-five.

"Which one? Danny? Or Bryce?"

"Mmmmm, Bryce. The delicious one." Bryce was a couple of years older than us. Danny was one year younger.

"Go on then, tell me all about it. How did it come about? When's the wedding?"

Time flew by as we gossiped, drank coffee, and

ate doughnuts. When Lani invited me to dinner, I gladly accepted—this was precisely what I needed, quality time with a good friend.

"Will Bryce be there?" I asked slyly.

"Nah, just me and Mom, I'm afraid. He's working tonight. But we should double date another time."

I snorted. "I'd need a date for that."

"I'm sure we can find you some hottie. You've been single too long."

"Yeah, well, life has been a little crazy, and I'm not sure anyone wants to get involved with a Shelton girl these days."

"That's bullshit. Anyone would be glad to have you. Look, hun, I gotta run. I was doing some errands for Ma. She's a little..." Lani broke off, and for a moment, I glimpsed something in her face.

"Hey, what's up? Is your mom okay?" Leaning forward, I placed my hand over hers on the table, and she turned her worried eyes to me.

"I think she may be getting Alzheimer's," Lani whispered. "Granddaddy had it. Ended up locked up in a home because he couldn't remember a damn thing and kept wandering off. We lost him for two whole days once. I can't bear to think of that happening to Mom."

"Oh, Lani, why didn't you tell me sooner?"

"None of it's confirmed. She won't go to the doctor's. But she forgets weird shit. You'll see it tonight. Come around six, and don't let on that I said anything, okay?"

***

WHAT DO you do when you think your best friend's mom is a ghoul? I've got no frigging clue, but I sensed that Lani's mom was not her mom the minute I stepped inside her house. The smell was different. The energy. She'd greeted me warmly enough with a smile and a "Hi, hun." But something was way off here, and it wasn't Alzheimer's.

"Is there anything I can do to help?" I offered, standing awkwardly in the kitchen and watching whoever this was parading as Mrs. B bustle about.

Anyone who knew me knew I was useless in the kitchen, and any offers of help were best declined. Lani opened her mouth, but I shushed her with a wave of my hand.

"Oh, bless you, I know you love to cook,"—she paused, and her eyes looked up at the ceiling for a moment before looking back at me—"Paige." She grinned, as if getting my name right was a moment of great triumph. "But I've got this all under control. Chicken casserole. Lani's favorite. You two run along, and I'll call you when it's ready."

Lani grabbed my wrist and dragged me from the kitchen and out onto the back porch, two beers in hand.

"See?" she hissed, tilting the bottle to her lips and taking a gulp. "She's not right in the head. Since when do you love to cook? Hell, it's always been an ongoing joke that you should be banned from every kitchen ever. And chicken casserole? My favorite? I detest it! Always have."

What could I say that would put my friend's mind at ease? That I thought maybe her mom was now a ghoul and not her mom at all—that she'd been... eaten? I couldn't do it. Clutching at straws, I tried my best to put a positive slant on the whole thing.

"Well, she does remember those things, just the wrong way around. She associates me with cooking and you with chicken." I shrugged. It was pretty flimsy, but it was all I had.

"I need to convince her to see a doctor," Lani declared.

"I guess." I felt awful. I didn't know how to help her, and seeing the pain in my friend's face made my heart ache. I needed to talk to Nate. He'd know what to do. We lapsed into silence, each lost in our own thoughts. Mine was turned toward her mom, as I'm sure Lani's was too, but I was wondering why she was targeted by a ghoul. And how? When did this happen, and why hadn't anyone noticed? Obviously, Lani was picking up on clues, minor things the ghoul had gotten wrong, but overall, whoever it was must have studied Mrs. B in advance or done some research at some point before—*gak*—consuming her. They'd slipped right into her life.

Another more worrying thought popped into my head. What if Lani insisted on dragging the meat bag she thought was her mom to the doctor? The ghoul wouldn't let that happen. They wouldn't let themselves be exposed, which meant Lani was in danger.

"How long has your mom had memory issues?" I asked.

"Started a couple of months ago," Lani replied. "Why?"

"No reason, just wondering." I shrugged. Two months ago. When the Gunslinger and Red Witch were in town. Was it linked?

"She'd gone to Redmeadows for a work

conference," Lani continued, twirling the beer bottle between her hands, "and came back different."

"She still work as a receptionist at...?" I was wracking my brain for the name of the firm when Lani supplied it.

"Stillwater Pharmaceuticals. Yeah. They're implementing a new software system or something, and Mom had to do the training. Since they had the big yearly conference in Redmeadows, they said she could go to that too. Learn more about the new product they're launching."

"She's been working there a long time, hasn't she?"

"About five years. Why? Oh my God!" Lani suddenly leaned toward me, grabbing my arm. "Do you think she's been exposed to something? At work? Some drug that has messed with her head?"

"Whoa, that's not what I'm saying at all," I protested. The last thing I wanted was Lani racing into the Stillwater offices, accusing them of anything. But I wanted to talk to Nate about this— the vampires had been in Maxxan to grow deadnettle for the drug Rampage. That operation had been shut down, but now a ghoul had taken up residence in the body of a pharmaceutical company's receptionist. Maybe it was a coincidence, or perhaps not, but worth looking into.

Dinner actually turned out to be an okay affair. Lani ate a lot of salad and bread, the chicken casserole was delicious, and we got caught up on old times, so I didn't notice Mrs. B's lack of interaction. Much.

It wasn't until I was leaving that I caught it. A sharp, intent look from Mrs. B, her brows pulled together in a tight frown before quickly smoothing away. Did the ghoul suspect that I suspected her? This whole thing gave me a headache, and my heart ached for what the future held for Lani. I couldn't allow this ghoul to continue masquerading as her mom, only right now, I was ill-equipped to deal with it. And, let's be honest, how do you tell your best friend that their mother has been eaten by a ghoul and not come across as sounding like a total lunatic? You don't.

I bid them both goodnight with a promise to catch up again soon and drove home thinking about my own mom. On impulse, I punched in her number, connecting the call through the car's Bluetooth.

"Paige, sweetheart, what's up?"

"Nothing, Mom. Just driving home from Lani's and thought I'd give you a call, check-in, you know."

"Oh, I haven't seen Lani in ages. How is she?" I spent the rest of the drive home gossiping with my mom, grateful beyond words that I was able to do such a thing.

ELEVEN

"Spitfire." Nate's voice on the line sent shivers down my spine. Delicious ones. I shrugged the sensation away and focused on the job at hand. I hadn't wanted to call him, but I was in over my head, and I knew it.

"I think my best friend's mom is a ghoul," I blurted.

"You think this why?" he asked. I told him everything about Lani and Mrs. B and then waited, holding my breath. He'd either laugh and tell me I had an overactive imagination, or he'd believe me.

"Give me the address." His voice was deadly serious. He believed me, which made it even more real, and while I rattled off Mrs. B's address, tears silently streamed down my cheeks. I didn't know what he was going to do, didn't want to know, and I disconnected the call without asking.

To calm my jumbled mind and fraught emotions, I ran a bath. A glance in the mirror confirmed my mascara had run down my face, and I absently ran my fingers under my eyes, smearing it even more. Sad panda, I said to myself. Tying my hair on top of my head, I went through my nightly skincare routine, cleansing my face thoroughly. Without makeup, my freckles were on full display across my nose. I touched my fingers to them. I'd always hated my freckles, the teasing at school, but as an adult, I'd discovered men actually liked them, liked to kiss them. Men, I'd decided, were weird.

Pouring a glass of wine, I sat it on the edge of the bath and stripped, tossing my clothes in the hamper before sliding into the fragrant hot water. Better. Much, much better.

I stayed in the bath until my fingers were pruned, and the water was cold. I felt marginally better. Pulling the plug, I wrapped a towel around myself and climbed out, more relaxed than earlier, but still worried. Very worried. Smearing myself in my favorite vanilla-scented body lotion, I moisturized my face and pulled on a long silk robe. Too wired for sleep, I fired up my laptop and typed in Stillwater Pharmaceuticals.

"You were right," a voice suddenly said behind me. I squealed, jumping up so fast I knocked my chair over, a fireball already balanced in the palm of my hand.

"Jesus!" I exclaimed. "Is this how it is with you? No knocking required?"

"Careful, don't want to burn your apartment down," Nate warned.

I extinguished the flame in my palm. "Well?" I demanded, wanting details.

Nate righted the chair. "I scouted around Mrs. B's place, and you are right. A ghoul is occupying the premises."

"Did you talk to her?"

"Didn't want to tip her off that we're on to her." Nate was shaking his head. "But the scent in and around the car and the front door is definitely ghoul. I caught your scent too, and a human girl."

"Lani." I nodded, tightening the belt on my robe and heading into the kitchen. "Want a drink?" I already had the bottle of wine in my hand and was refilling my glass when I thought to offer him one.

"Sure." Pouring him a glass, I handed it to him before sinking down onto the sofa.

"What's next then?"

"I want you to check out the house. Tomorrow, when she goes to work."

"What will you be doing?"

"Staying out of the sun." His reply was droll, and I shot him a sharp look. "I'll be researching Stillwater Pharmaceuticals and also the tracking device we put on the car. Run down any leads on Byers," he added.

"To be clear, you want me to break in? To Mrs. B's house?"

"Correct."

"And what am I looking for?"

"Anything out of the ordinary."

"Well, that narrows it down." I cradled my wine. "What if I get caught?"

"Tell them you forgot something...left something behind when you went to dinner. Come on, Paige, you know how to do this. You've been hunting vampires for weeks."

"I was luring them to the warehouse and killing them," I protested, "not breaking into their homes and snooping."

"Surely the latter is preferable? Less...deadly." I swear he was laughing under his breath at me. My temper flared, and a fission of electricity buzzed over my skin. Then, just as quickly as it had arrived, it disappeared, and a mischievous impulse surged through me. Placing my glass on the coffee table, I turned to him, splaying my hands across his chest, seeing his eyes widen.

"Let's dance," I suggested, reaching for the stereo remote and hitting play.

"What?" He sounded confused, and I smiled. I had him exactly where I wanted him. On the back foot. Let's see how he liked it for a change.

Standing, I pulled him to his feet and brought him closer until our bodies touched and my breasts rubbed against him. Then I gave a slow twist of my hips against his.

His arms tightened around me, yanking me to him until we were molded together. One hand crept up to tug my head back, and I smiled smugly at him.

"How does it feel not to know what the hell is going on?"

My body was still curled around him, taunting him. This was so unlike me, playing with fire, teasing him in this way. The heat in his eyes should have warned me to quit while I was ahead, but all it did was entice me.

"Playing with fire, Spitfire?" His mouth grazed my cheek as he spoke directly in my ear, his lips warm against my skin. My head spun, my senses reeled, and in reply, my lips pressed against his neck. I felt the shudder that ran through him. Then his body ground into mine, jerking my head back with a thick handful of hair until our eyes locked. What had started out as a game was now an open challenge, as well as a direct threat.

His mouth came down onto mine. It had been so long since I'd kissed someone, and it hadn't been an act. A trick to lure them in. His tongue caressed my lips before twining around mine and seeking to explore my mouth with a thorough intensity.

He broke away, cupped my face in his hands, and pinned me with eyes afire with passion. "I can't take much more of this," he ground out, his eyes dropping to my mouth and then back up to my eyes. "You need to decide if this is what you want, because I'm very close to making your mind up for you."

My body was screaming with lust. There wasn't a single part of me that didn't want to throw him to the floor and ravish him—repeatedly.

"Nate…" I couldn't put it into words, couldn't voice the need I had for him. He mistook my hesitation and set me away from him with firm hands on my shoulders.

"Get some rest. When you come to me, and you will, it will be willingly." I opened my mouth to argue, but he was gone. I'd never get used to the speed vampires could move. With his commanding presence removed, reality crashed back in. Now was not the time or place to be indulging in my fantasies over Nate Wilder—never mind the fact I was second-guessing myself at having any feelings at all for a vampire.

But he was right. My body clock was all over the place, working nights with him, days on my business. I was exhausted, and the knowledge that Mrs. B had been eaten by ghouls was eating me up inside. I needed a clear head to deal with whatever tomorrow had to bring.

And I had a feeling it was going to be a doozy.

TURNED OUT I WAS WRONG.

Heading out to Mrs. B's house after ten, knowing she usually started her shift as a receptionist at

Stillwater Pharmaceuticals at nine, I parked down the street and approached on foot, just in case she was at home unexpectedly. My luck held. Her car wasn't in the driveway. Using the spare key she'd kept under a flower pot since the days when Lani and I were kids, I let myself in and began the search. I had no clue what I was looking for and didn't turn up anything out of the ordinary. Everything was the same, just as I'd remembered it growing up. I'd spent hours in this house, playing with Lani as kids, hanging out as teenagers. It was all so familiar, but now I was looking at it with different eyes. Suspicious eyes. I rubbed at the ache in my chest, knowing the real Mrs. B was dead.

With the house search a bust, I returned to my car and pondered what to do next. It was past lunchtime, and Nate would probably be sleeping by now. I had hours to kill, and I couldn't let this go, couldn't sit and do nothing while some asshole was walking around in my best friend's mom's skin.

Starting the car, I pulled out and headed toward Stillwater Pharmaceuticals. I had no reason to be there and hadn't come up with a reasonable cover story by the time I pulled into the parking lot, so I merely sat in the car and watched. The building was massive. A small modern office at the front, all glass, and sleek white surfaces, then at the rear, towering up over the landscape, were the factory and warehouse. All I knew about the company was that they manufactured a range of drugs here. Not the everyday painkiller type stuff you can buy off the shelf. Specialist drugs. For the treatments of cancers and acute illnesses. I thought I remembered Mrs. B said that they were branching out into vaccinations, but I couldn't recall the details. I'd never paid much attention to her work before, and I was kicking myself now because that sort of info would have been invaluable.

Blowing out a breath, I peered at the reception area. The head I could see through the window did not belong to Mrs. B. Someone else was manning the reception desk. Maybe Mrs. B was on a bathroom break or something? I continued to wait and watch. Mrs. B did not put in an appearance. I was about to leave when a door to the right opened, and Mrs. B strode into view. I'd never seen her walk with such confidence, such purpose. She had on a white lab coat, and I frowned. The new Mrs. B clearly wasn't a receptionist anymore.

With my bladder fit to burst and my stomach growling, I finally called it quits and headed home. Today didn't feel like such a bust after all. Only I didn't know what any of it meant—if any of this was relevant at all. Maybe Mrs. B had simply stumbled upon the path of a hungry ghoul, and it was poor misfortunate luck. No conspiracy. Nothing. Urgh, I hated second-guessing myself like this!

After a quick refresh and late lunch, I settled into work, glad of the distraction since I was giving myself a headache trying to guess what on earth was going on in Maxxan. My work held my attention only for so long, and then I found I was mindlessly scrolling through social media, wasting time, when there was a knock at the door.

"So, you do know how to knock?" Holding the door open, I stood to one side to let Nate in. I hadn't noticed it had grown dark.

"How did the house search go?" he asked.

"Didn't find a thing. I went out to the factory—"

"What?" he interrupted, and I held up a hand.

"Calm down. I stayed in the car. Mrs. B wasn't at reception, which is interesting because she was a receptionist before she was a ghoul. Wait, that didn't come out right."

"I know what you mean." He waved a hand to indicate I keep talking.

"I caught sight of her in a lab coat," I quickly finished.

"Interesting. Get changed." He settled on my sofa to wait while I stood in the middle of my lounge room and frowned.

"Changed? Into what? Not more hunting!"

"I thought you'd be keen to hunt." Again, his lips were twitching, and my annoyance skyrocketed.

"Not when I'm distracted. My head has to be in the game for a successful hunt."

"At least you're not entirely foolish." He nodded as if pleased.

"Hey!" I protested at his backhanded compliment.

"We're breaking into the Stillwater factory. Wear something dark. Flat shoes...if you own any." His eyes dropped to my stilettoes. These were purple, to match my dress. Another swirly one with pockets.

"Cat burglarish?"

"Purrfect."

Ignoring his pun, I hurried into my bedroom, firmly closing the door and kicking off my heels. I had one pair of runners. My Nikes. I dug out my black yoga pants and a black tank and braided my hair. Examining myself in the mirror, I nodded and returned to the living room where Nate waited.

"Did you find anything today?" I asked.

"I did. The car Ian had been driving turned up at the factory yesterday and hasn't moved since."

"Wow, what a coincidence." Sarcasm rolled off my tongue, but he ignored it.

"Let's go."

At the factory, Nate stopped the car almost a mile back from the gate. "We'll walk from here."

Climbing out, I followed him. He kept to a self-made path running parallel to the road—easy to duck behind a tree or bush should anyone drive past.

"It's still pretty early," I commented. "Won't people be around?" It was just past eight o'clock.

"There are always people around in a facility like this. Makes no difference if it's seven in the evening or two in the morning. The fact is, if they're expecting trouble, they'd expect it in the early hours of the morning."

"Oh. Makes sense." I'd never thought of it that way before.

"No more talking. Voices carry."

We were approaching the parking lot I'd been in earlier. The gates were now closed, and a high chain-link fence surrounding the parking lot and buildings prevented trespassers.

"Here," Nate whispered, crouched at the base of

the fence with his hands cupped together, waiting for my foot. Hesitantly, I lifted my leg and placed my foot in his hands. "I'm going to hoist you up—fast. Vault over. Don't squeal."

"I don't squeal," I protested, clamping my lips together when he frowned at me.

"One. Two." On three, he shunted me into the air, and I almost screamed. Even though I'd been expecting it, I hadn't expected to go so high, so fast. The top of the fence was covered in razor wire, so I had to angle my body to clear the top without touching—which was actually easy since I flew about twenty feet higher than necessary. I landed with a thump, and the air whooshed from my lungs. My feet felt like they'd shattered inside my Nikes, but I didn't squeal.

Nate landed by my side.

"Okay?"

"Mmmhmmm." I grimaced, ignoring the pain in my feet. Any broken bones would heal, as would any soft tissue damage.

"Good. Right, we're heading around the back to the loading dock. I can bypass the security on the door there."

"You know how to bypass security?"

"Remember when I told you I'd been a soldier, a

marine, a navy seal, special ops? I've got skills." Keeping low, he headed across the parking lot, keeping to the shadows and avoiding the scattering of parking lot lights. I followed, a little slower and trying to hide my limp. He noticed.

"Why didn't you tell me you were hurt?" Swinging me up into his arms before I could so much as open my mouth, he carried me the rest of the way, moving so fast my eyes watered. At the rear of the warehouse, he set me on my feet, frowning.

"Did you sprain your ankle?"

"Broke a few bones, I think," I muttered, rotating one foot, then the other.

"Both? Fuck."

"Let me try something. Can you take my shoes off for me? I'm going to try to flame just my feet. Heal them."

"You can do that?" Dropping to one knee, he lifted my left foot, undid the laces, and carefully slid the shoe off. Blood dripped, and he sucked in a breath.

"That had to have hurt." There was a rumble in his voice, a growl, and I wondered if my blood was too much of a temptation.

"You're not going to bite me, are you?" I asked.

"Not without you asking me to." He busied

himself removing my other shoe, then looked up at me, waiting.

"Stand back a bit, so you don't get burned," I ordered, then concentrated on calling forth my flame but concentrating solely on my feet. If I flamed all over, my clothes would be ruined, and I really didn't want to be breaking into anywhere naked.

"Well, look at that."

It worked. My feet flamed as far as the ankle and stopped. I felt the bones realign; the tendons pull back together, and within seconds, I was healed.

Before I could stop him, Nate was kneeling at my feet once more, easing each foot back into its respective shoe. I tried to hide my sudden breathlessness at the touch of his fingers on my skin, the way he gently cradled my foot, which looked incredibly small in the palm of his hand, and eased my shoe back on. I had a very new appreciation for Cinderella.

"I'm sorry you got hurt. That was my fault. I didn't consider the impact the landing would have on you." His face was close to mine, and I couldn't think; just stare into his stormy gray eyes and blink. He smiled and backed away.

"Let's do this. Stay behind me." He vaulted up

onto a platform behind us, leaned down, and held out his hand to haul me up. As soon as I was next to him, he released me and turned to the keypad on the wall. Within a matter of seconds, there was a buzz, and the light turned green. We were in. Nate Wilder was proving handy to have around.

S lipping inside, I immediately plastered my back to the wall and shuffled along until I could duck behind a shelving unit for cover. It was dark, the only light coming from the glass panel in a doorway directly opposite. Nate pressed in behind me, surveying the area.

"Dispatch," he whispered into my ear. Distracted by the warmth of his breath, it took me a couple of seconds to realize he was telling me we were in the dispatch room, where whatever it was that was produced here was packaged and ready for delivery.

"Right," I eventually replied, wriggling away from his distracting presence.

"I want to see the labs. Find out what they're really working on here."

"You don't think it's the cancer treatments they claim?"

"Oh, I'm sure they do produce those, too, but I think there's something else beneath the surface."

I was just about to step out and head toward the door on the opposite side of the room when he grabbed my wrist. "Wait! Cameras." He pointed, indicating two cameras in opposite corners covering the room. Damn.

"Wait here. I can put all the cameras in this place on a loop; then we can move around freely."

"Won't they see you?"

"I'll be fast." He winked and was gone, moving faster than I'd ever seen—or, more correctly, not seen. Rather than a blur, he was a puff of wind. Invisible.

Less than a minute later, he was back. "Right. Cameras are no longer a problem. But there are security guards and some people working late, so we need to be careful. I'd rather they not know we were here."

"Right." My heart was pounding in my chest, and I sucked in a deep breath to try to steady the wave of anxiety that pulsed through me. This was real. This was dangerous. I'd faced vampires without fear, yet breaking into this place with the knowledge that it was either run by ghouls or ghouls were involved scared the ever-living daylights out of me.

Nate must have been able to hear the frantic beating of my heart, but he didn't call me out on it; just told me to stay close as he headed back the way he'd come at a more civilized pace.

We'd searched a couple of labs without turning up anything unusual. Nate gave me a list of drugs that he knew were legitimate, and I compared them with the vials I found in the glass-fronted refrigerators. They were a match, nothing out of the ordinary. In the third lab, we hit pay dirt. None of the drugs in the fridge were on my list.

"Found something," I whispered, knowing his vamp ears could easily hear me. "These aren't on the list. The label says Anate."

"I knew it. This is it. I'm going to take a sample. Keep looking to see if you can find anything else."

I did what I'd wanted to do ever since we'd broken in. Turning to a computer, I wriggled the mouse to wake it up, pleased that whoever had used it last hadn't even logged out, let alone turned it off. Which meant one thing. They were still here. We'd have to hurry.

"This computer is still logged in," I told Nate. "I'm going to do some digging, but I think whoever logged in is probably still in the building—they'd have protocols to follow. No one would leave without properly logging out."

"Correct. Be quick."

I began typing, searching for HR records. I'd just pulled up Mrs. B's file when Nate opened the refrigerator door and removed a vial. Alarms blared, and I jumped in fright.

"Damn it," he cursed, "the door has a trigger. Clever bastards."

Ignoring him, I quickly scanned Mrs. B's info while Nate grabbed handfuls of the vials and shoved them into the cargo pockets of his pants. Mrs. B was now a project manager, promoted when she returned from Redmeadows, working on Project Anate.

I was still reading when Nate grabbed my wrist and dragged me back toward the door. "We're out of time."

Then I could hear it too. Pounding footsteps. Running towards us. We cleared the door. It hadn't even clicked shut behind us when Nate swung me up into his arms and propelled us out of the building, over the fence, and back to the car in the space of a heartbeat. I was shaking when he set me down by the vehicle.

"Okay?"

I must have looked as green as I felt. I nodded, not trusting myself to speak in case I hurled over his shoes. I was never any fun on carnival rides thanks to my motion sickness, and that quick joyride had my stomach churning.

"Get in." Opening the door, he stood back and allowed me to climb inside under my own steam. I closed my eyes, leaning my head back, and concentrated on breathing. The car started, he spun us around, and we were off.

"Why so fast?" I asked, not opening my eyes. "They didn't see us, can't identify us."

"No, but I don't think it will take them long to figure out you were involved."

"How?"

"Because you were looking at Mrs. B's info. Who else would break in, steal drugs, and look up one particular person's file? You were at her house recently. You said that she'd given you an odd look —maybe she suspected you were on to her even then."

"Fuck," I whispered.

"Exactly. You've been compromised. I need to

get you out of here." Nate was driving like a maniac, but even though the speed was beyond fast, he had complete control of the car, and surprisingly, I wasn't yelling at him, demanding that he slow down.

"What's the plan?" I knew he'd have one. He was the type who had a plan for a plan.

"Pack a bag. We're leaving." He swung in behind my apartment with a squeal of tires. "I'm arranging transport."

I didn't argue, merely flung open the door and hurried upstairs. I pulled my suitcase from the closet and piled clothes in with no regard for their welfare. One part of me cried at how I was treating my designer threads; the other side knew I didn't have time to even think about it. We needed to leave. Now. My sense of self-preservation was high, and fear was forcing my blood pressure through the roof. Snatching up my laptop and shoving it into my bag, I hefted the satchel over my shoulder and was out the door, banging the suitcase down the stairs behind me.

Nate met me at the bottom and stowed the case in the trunk without a word. His silence drilled home the gravity of my situation. We were in danger. The fact that he was evacuating me out of

Maxxan spoke volumes. Shit had just got real, and the game I'd thought I'd been playing had turned sinister. Climbing back into the car, I put on my seatbelt and watched as he shoved the car into gear, turned off the headlights, and peeled out like the hounds of hell were after us.

"A chopper is on the way. It'll pick us up at Rae's place; less chance of being detected out there."

"Right." I wanted to sound as cool and calm as he was, but my voice betrayed me, the quiver giving away just how scared I was. His agitation was adding to my own nerves. If someone like Nate Wilder was worried, then we were in deep trouble.

His hand landed on my knee and squeezed. "It's going to be okay," he reassured me.

"I know." I tried to smile but failed. Pretty sure I was just baring my teeth at him. He chuckled.

"Would you mind driving with both hands on the wheel?" At the speeds he was driving, it wouldn't take much to lose control and flip.

"Don't trust me?"

"Eyes on the road."

He chuckled again but humored me, removing his hand from my knee, returning it to the wheel, and facing front again. I released the breath I'd been holding.

It usually took me twenty minutes to drive to Rae's place. We made it in ten. Nate stowed the car in the garage, plucked my suitcase from the trunk, and hustled me to the back of the house.

"Do you think they know about this place?" I asked, standing in the moonlight, my heart a wreck in my chest. I looked back at Grandma's house. They'd better not touch it, I vowed, or I'd come back and rip their sorry hearts from their chests. Brave words for a vampire hunter who was currently scared shitless and trembling in her boots.

"Doubtful. The chopper will be here soon. How are you holding up?"

Throughout all of this, despite it, I felt safe with him. It was illuminating. Without noticing it, trusting Nate had snuck up on me. Despite the attraction I was resisting so valiantly. Despite all my misgivings. I trusted him to keep me safe.

"I'm fine. I'm sorry I got us busted." If I'd known he was going to drag me away, I would have made sure I'd exited out of Mrs. B's records, but as it was, her picture had been smiling at me from the screen as I'd been pulled away.

"It was me who got us busted," he corrected. "I didn't think to look for an alarm on the refrigerator door. Clever. A level of security going beyond the norm."

"You got plenty of samples, though, right? I saw you stuffing them in your pockets. They won't break, will they?"

"These pockets are lined with Mylar."

"What's Mylar?"

"That silver stuff you find inside insulated bags. It'll keep them cool, and it's waterproof should they leak or break."

It appeared the SIA had thought of everything. Sitting on the back porch, I stared into the darkness, seeing nothing, my mind going over everything we'd learned. Our search for one ghoul had led us to accidentally discover my best friend's mom was now a ghoul and worked at Stillwater Pharmaceuticals. People were going missing. It wasn't a stretch to imagine Stillwater was using them in some sort of illegal experiment. And if they had to dispose of bodies, ghouls were an excellent way to do it. My stomach churned, and I blinked rapidly to still the sudden urge to vomit.

"You okay?" Nate sat next to me, close but not quite touching.

"Struggling to get my head around the ghouls," I admitted. It was only a few days ago when I'd been merrily hunting vampires and feeling pretty cocky at my own prowess. Now I was not only working with one, but I was starting to trust him, and worse, like him. All my life, I'd listened to my dad and uncles telling us how awful vampires were. They'd killed Grandpa. Hurt Rae. They were evil bloodsucking creatures who must be destroyed. Yet here I was, joining forces with the very being I'd sworn to kill and discovering that maybe, just maybe, everything I'd been told as a child was wrong.

"Could I make a call?" I needed to talk to Rae.

"Sure."

I moved away so he couldn't overhear and then laughed at myself. I could stand two miles away, and he'd still be able to hear if he put his mind to it. Sensing my need for privacy, Nate stood. "I'm going to check the perimeter. I won't listen in."

"Can vampires read minds?"

"No. But I can read you like a book." With that, he was gone, and I was standing in the moonlight, the sound of crickets chirping and a soft breeze ruffling my hair. So peaceful yet at total odds with the anxiety churning inside.

I dialed.

Rae answered after one ring. "Paige, how're things? I hear you mastered flaming brilliantly."

"Yeah. Good." Should have known Nate had kept her updated. I cleared my throat. "I wanted to...ask you something...talk to you about something..."

"Sure, what's up?"

"You remember growing up and our dads drumming into us that vampires are bad, evil bloodsuckers?"

"Ahhhh. Nate Wilder." I could picture Rae nodding, a brief smile crossing her face. "You're conflicted? Confused?"

"All of those things," I whispered.

"Okay, let me lay it out for you." Rae blew out a breath. "Our dads, our parents, thought they were doing the right thing. Grandpa was killed by vampires, it's true, but what they didn't know, and neither did we until recently, is that there are your average everyday vampires, and then there are rogues. Rogues are the deadly ones, the ones who've gone off the reservation—for whatever reason. They kill for fun, for sport, for food. They can't control their bloodlust—for whatever reason. Some of them, it's just their nature. They were probably addicts or had issues as humans, which carried over into their vampire life when they turned. Others were adversely affected by Rampage, turning them into blood-crazy vamps that can't be controlled."

"I didn't trust Nate at all when I started with the SIA, even though I had Jordan's word that he was a stand-up guy. Yes, he's rich, handsome, successful, powerful. That doesn't mean he can't be a douche. Then I came here for training and worked with him one-on-one and got to know him. He's an okay guy, Paige. In fact, I've met a lot of vampires now, and they are all decent people.

"Our dads didn't know better because the one who was meant to teach them about their heritage, their fire demon powers, and all the supernatural stuff didn't. I don't know why Grandpa didn't give them that knowledge when they first came into their fire demon powers at eighteen. We'll never know. He took those answers to the grave. When he was killed, our dads just assumed that all vampires were evil. And taught us that, too."

I was silent, digesting what she'd said. It was true. We had inherited our parents' prejudices, but it was hard to shake when it was all you had known ever since you were a child.

"You still there?" Rae asked.

"Yeah, sorry. I'm here."

"I wouldn't have given Nate access to the house if I didn't trust him."

"I kinda figured that, but didn't want to believe it," I admitted.

"You can trust him, Paige."

"I'm not sure it's that easy." I caught movement at the corner of my eye and saw Nate returning, pointing at the sky. "I've gotta go. Thanks for the talk." I hung up and waited for Nate.

"Chopper's coming in. Can you light up to guide it in?"

"Oh. Sure." Following him to a clearing away from the house, I stood and waited until I could hear the helicopter myself and then lit up both palms and waved them over my head. The wind whipped dust up around me, and I squeezed my eyes shut but kept my fire burning until the helicopter was almost upon me. Extinguishing the flame, I moved back a few feet and watched as it landed, a big black machine, large rotors whipping the air with a *whomp, whomp, whomp.*

"Come on," Nate shouted over the noise. He opened the rear door and threw my suitcase inside, then held his hand out to me. I placed my hand in his and let him help me on board. I'd never ridden in a helicopter before. I was amped on adrenaline and more than a little apprehension.

"Here." Looming over me, Nate snapped a

harness over my shoulders and around my waist, then slipped a headset over my ears. I saw him place my satchel beneath the seat opposite me and realized I'd totally forgotten to pick it up. I flashed him a grateful smile. I'd have been as pissed as hell if I'd left my laptop behind.

"It'll take us a couple of hours to get to Redmeadows." Nate's voice came through the headset, and I swiveled my head to look at him. I hadn't even noticed when he'd sat next to me and strapped himself in. There were six seats in the rear of the helicopter, two sets of three facing each other. He could have sat anywhere, but he sat next to me. When the helicopter jolted and started to rise, I sucked in a breath and spun my head to look out the window again, a shiver of nerves tightening my stomach.

"Breathe. You'll be fine. It's a perfectly safe way to travel." His fingers wrapped around mine, and instead of snatching my hand away, I squeezed in thanks. For once, I was grateful for his presence. Rae's words were still swirling around in my brain, and I knew she wasn't feeding me bullshit. I was safe with Nate, and I could trust him.

The helicopter lifted up higher and higher and pitched to the left. I squeezed his hand tighter, and he gave me a squeeze back. I didn't dare look at him for fear he was laughing at me.

"Paige?"

"Hmmm?"

"Look at me." The way he said it, not an order, more of a request, had me obeying. I looked into those mesmerizing stormy gray eyes and felt like I was drowning, being sucked into a whirlpool that I feared I'd never resurface from.

"Why are you so scared?" He raised a hand to trace his finger over my cheek, and I shivered.

"I'm not scared," I lied.

"Liar." The corner of his lip curled, and my eyes zeroed in, my tongue stroking along my lower lip as I absently remembered the taste of his kiss.

"I've never ridden in a helicopter before," I said breathlessly.

"That's not what's got you all worked up." The timbre of his voice was low, vibrating through me. At that moment, I wished nothing more than to forget my past, my hate of vampires, and throw myself at him to quench the curiosity and undeniable attraction burning through me. I hesitated, wanting to lean forward and touch my lips to his, but another part held back, unsure if I wanted to go down this path.

THIRTEEN

The seconds stretched on, the silence heavy, until he blinked, looked beyond me into the dark night outside the window, and then leaned back as if that intimate moment hadn't happened. Leaving me more confused than ever.

I hadn't noticed him bringing a bag on board, so when he rummaged inside a backpack and withdrew a laptop, I couldn't help but stare. He busied himself with what I could only assume was SIA business. I must have dozed off because the next thing I knew, Nate was shouting, slamming the laptop shut, and grabbing my arm.

"What's happening?" I blinked, groggy. Alarms

were blaring from the cockpit, and the helicopter suddenly swung around, its tail spinning us in wild, crazy circles.

"We're going down!" the pilot yelled.

"What? We're what?" I screamed, clutching at Nate, who was in the process of releasing his safety belt. "What are you doing? Strap yourself in!"

"We're going to crash. Brace yourself." Before I could ask what in the hell he was talking about, he was out of his seat and draped over me, his arms wrapping around my headrest, so my face was buried in his chest, his knees clamped tight on either side of my hips. He was shielding me. Protecting me.

We went down fast, yet it happened in slow motion. The sound of the engine whining, the blades slicing through the air, but only succeeding in spinning us in dizzying circles on a downward trajectory. I could barely breathe with my face pressed into Nate's chest, but that didn't matter; since I was screaming long and loud, I didn't have time to breathe, anyway.

Then we made impact, and my screams stopped as we bounced and rolled along the ground, the terrifying sounds of metal ripping apart, the silence from the engine, the whoosh as the propeller was torn from the body and flung off into god only knew where. Outside, I could see nothing but darkness—at least we hadn't landed on someone's house. A strange thought when you're bouncing uncontrollably in a crashed helicopter.

Eventually, we skidded to a halt.

"Oh, God," I whimpered. I was upside down, dangling from my safety harness. I couldn't see Nate at all. Had he been flung out? With shaking fingers, I pressed the release button on my harness, but nothing happened. Frantically, I pushed at it again and again, but it was jammed, and I was stuck. With my blood rushing to my head, it was hard to think beyond the panic thrumming through my veins.

"Nate?" I called, then stilled my struggles to listen intently. Nothing. Not a sound. It was eerily silent. "Mr. Pilot?" I tried. We'd never been introduced; I'd only caught a glimpse of the man behind the controls when he'd landed at Rae's house. No answer. Was I here alone?

Minutes ticked by, and my head ached from hanging upside down. There were no voices outside, no one calling out. It was just me. With a sob, I wrapped my hand around the release buckle and concentrated, directing my heat to the clasp. I knew it would hurt as the plastic and metal became heated and seared into my palm, but it was the only way I could think of to get out. I didn't want to risk an open flame in case aviation fuel had sprayed throughout the cabin—I could accidentally blow myself up.

"Argh!" The metal buckle burned and melted into my palm, branding me, but I held tight until it completely fell away. I collapsed to the floor on my hands and knees and immediately crawled to the shattered window, wriggling my way out of the narrow gap and onto the grass outside.

It was pitch black, and my hand hurt like a bitch. Calling forth my flame, I healed myself, then called forth a fireball to use as a light. What I saw had me swearing. The helicopter was a mess, nothing but a crushed ball. There was barely anything left of it. I hurried around to the front and peered inside. The pilot was there, in his seat, a metal rod protruding from his chest all the way through the windshield. Hurrying around to his window, I reached in and felt for a pulse. He was dead.

"Nate!" Straightening, I cupped my hands around my mouth and yelled. Nothing. Where the hell was he? I could see the path of destruction the helicopter had taken as it plowed across the land, and with my flame to light the way, I traced the route back, calling out to Nate as I went. He had to be here, somewhere.

"Paige." It was barely a whisper, but I heard it. Stopping, I swiveled, looking into the undergrowth. We'd landed in some sort of woods or forest, trees as far as the eye could see. I guess they broke our fall somewhat.

"Nate! Where are you?"

"Here." A little louder, I was getting closer. I started to run, desperate to get to him. He had to be hurt; otherwise, he would have come for me. I practically tripped over him, he was lying so still in the grass.

"Shit." Kneeling by his side, I called more flame and ran my hand over his body. His injury was apparent. Like the pilot, Nate sported a metal pole pinning him to the ground. "Here, let me." I had to extinguish my flame to wrap both hands around the bar. Before I could pull, Nate stopped me. "Careful. It's resting against my heart. Pull slowly and carefully."

"No pressure," I whispered, my palms suddenly

sweating and slippery. Inch by inch, I eased the pole out of his chest, wincing at the squelching noise it made and doing my best to ignore Nate's occasional hiss of pain. This had to hurt like the devil. Finally, after what felt like an eternity, the pole was free, and I tossed it aside. Holding another fireball, I watched as his flesh knitted back together. Then I burst into tears.

"Hey now, what's all this?" he chided, sitting up and wrapping his arms around me. I dropped the fireball, and it went out, leaving us in darkness. I couldn't stop the tears now that they'd started. Rather than telling me to pull myself together, he rubbed a hand up and down my back in a soothing gesture and kept whispering over and over that it was okay and we were safe.

Eventually, my hysterics subsided, and embarrassment settled in. I'd never been much of a crier and hated it when people saw me cry. It made me feel weak. I pushed away from him and wiped my arm over my eyes.

"Sorry," I mumbled, mortified.

"It's okay. You needed the release." Jumping to his feet, he held out a hand and hauled me up next to him. I couldn't help but notice he swayed a little.

"Are you okay?"

"I need to feed. Healing took a lot out of me."

"Oh." I shifted my weight from foot to foot, knowing what I had to do, but incredibly unsure. Eventually, I held out my wrist and said, "Here."

He chuckled. "Spitfire, if I drink your blood, it won't be from your wrist." He began walking, calling over his shoulder, "I'll be okay. You don't have to make the ultimate sacrifice for me. I know it makes you uncomfortable."

I hurried after him. "But you need to feed!"

"I'll survive." Ignoring me, he kept moving, and I dutifully followed. It wasn't until I'd stumbled and fallen for the third time that he stopped.

"This isn't working," he observed.

"No shit. I can't fucking see. It's okay for you with your vampy super fucking vision, but for me, it's like walking blindfolded." Despite having a glowing ball of fire in my palm to guide the way, I could only see a couple of feet in front of me. My frustration was boiling over, and I knew without seeing that he was laughing at me.

"Damn." There was rustling, and then he was right in my face. "Wait here. I'm going ahead to scout out some shelter. I can't be out here when dawn hits, especially in my weakened state."

Oh, man, didn't I feel like an asshole? I'd

forgotten he wouldn't be able to tolerate the sunlight. Here I'd been cursing him for making me walk through the dark when he had no other option. I hung my head in shame.

"I'm sorry. I didn't even think of that." My apology went unanswered. He was long gone, leaving me standing alone in the dark. I kept going in the general direction we'd been heading. I refused to stand out here like a useless female and wait for him to come back for me.

Thunder rumbled overhead, and I glanced up. That would explain the lack of moonlight or stars. A storm was covering the sky. In the distance, a fork of lightning lit up the night momentarily before plunging me back into darkness. I counted in my head until the thunder rumbled again. Close. The storm was close, yet another reason why shelter was a mighty fine idea.

Plunging on, I peered ahead as best I could. I should have scouted the helicopter for a torch. While my flame was handy, it didn't have the same penetration as a beam of light.

I'd been alone, struggling over the uneven terrain for at least an hour when the downpour started. Within seconds I was drenched, and try as I might, I couldn't keep my flame alight. Water dripping in my eyes, I raised an arm to shield my face and kept moving forward, only now I was virtually blind, and I had no idea what direction Nate had gone. I'd thought I'd been traveling in a straight line, but who knew? And as much as I groused that I didn't want him to return to rescue me, I actually did. I was starting to get worried. Had he left me out here alone? I had no idea where we were or how far away from civilization we were. I wasn't equipped for this. Small mercy I was wearing my trainers and not heels; that's all I can say.

It wasn't until I almost walked into it that I discovered I'd cleared the forest, and there was a structure looming up in front of me. Reaching my hands out, I slowly shuffled forward until I touched it. Wood. Okay, maybe a house or a barn. Yet it was still pitch black. The wind had picked up now, and I was starting to shiver in my wet clothes. This barn —or whatever it was—couldn't have come at a better time.

Keeping one hand on the wooden siding, I felt along until I came to a corner, turned, and continued the process until my hand fell away to nothing. A door. An open door! Halleluiah! Stepping inside, I shook the water off my arms and summoned my fire, holding it high in my palm. I looked around. Yep, a barn. Old and abandoned by the looks of things. Rain dripped through in a couple of places, but other than that, it was dry. There were some old hay bales off to one side, a pile of junk, and a shit ton of cobwebs. And no Nate.

"Where are you?" I spoke out loud as if expecting an answer. None was forthcoming. I'd found this place by accident. So we must be on someone's property. Maybe there was a house nearby, and Nate had found his way there. Returning to the doorway, I stood and looked at the torrential rain and decided I'd stay put, at least until the rain stopped.

Making a clearing and piling together some wooden crates, I set them on fire, careful to keep the flames contained lest I burn down my shelter. With the fire merrily dancing away and providing plenty of light and warmth, I stretched my hands out to it and puzzled over what to do next. I wasn't SIA trained. I wasn't a camper either. I had no clue what to do out here in the middle of nowhere. And I didn't want to examine too closely my niggling worry over Nate. He was a vampire, a powerful one. He could take care of himself. But he'd sustained a horrific injury, one that had drained him when he'd healed. What if he hadn't found...food? What if he was lying out there, hurt? Dying?

"Fuck it." Striding to the door, I peered outside. I'd come from the left, but straight ahead, through the fall of water...was that a boot on the ground? I stretched my neck, narrowed my eyes, but couldn't tell for sure.

"This had better be worth it, Wilder," I fumed, stepping out into the rain again and heading toward where I thought I'd seen a man's boot. Turned out I was right. Lying face down in the rain was a man, all in black. From this angle, I couldn't tell if it was Nate or not, but he looked to be his height and build, and who else could it possibly be? Rolling him over, I sucked in a breath. It was Nate, all right. He was out cold. His face was white, and his cheeks were sunken. He must have found the barn and had been returning for me when he ran out of juice.

Grabbing both of his feet, I dragged him back to the barn, puffing at the weight of him. I was wheezing by the time I got him inside and over by the fire. Dragging him over the mud had forced his shirt up around his chest, and I got an uninterrupted view of his abs. I couldn't help myself; I reached out a hand and placed my palm flat on them, expecting a response from him, stunned when there was none.

"Nate?" Now I was really worried. Tugging his shirt down, I scrambled up toward his head and, with trembling fingers, felt for a pulse. Barely there. But he was alive, just. I'd always thought vampires were the living dead, but he'd educated me on that. Their hearts still beat, and blood still pumped through their bodies. They just needed to replenish that blood on a regular basis.

Clearly, Nate needed blood, and he needed it now. Jumping to my feet, I searched the barn for something to cut myself with, but came up empty. I briefly toyed with the idea of using my own teeth but quickly scrapped it. I'd never go through with it, no matter how badly he needed blood. Which left Nate himself. He was SIA. Surely, he had a weapon of some sort on him. Patting him down, I ran my palms over his thighs, searched the pockets of his trousers. It wasn't until I reached his boots that I found a small blade tucked inside a hidden sheath on the inside of his boot.

The storm had picked up intensity outside, and it seemed fitting to have the wild soundtrack of Mother Nature booming around me as I contemplated the unthinkable. I was about to slit my wrist and feed a vampire. With a self-deprecating laugh, I drew the blade across my flesh, sucking in a breath at the sting, then quickly holding my wrist over his mouth as the blood dripped.

"Drink," I whispered. For a second, I didn't think it had worked, for the blood fell on him, hitting his lips and sliding down his chin and across his cheeks with no reaction from him. Then he stirred. His tongue appeared to swipe at his bottom lip, then his eyes flashed open, and his mouth was clamped to my wrist so fast I hadn't seen him move. I gasped when his fangs pierced my flesh, the pain burning. He was pulling at my wrist, sucking the blood from my veins faster than it could pump out.

As suddenly as it had started, he stopped, frozen, his mouth at my wrist, his eyes on mine. I watched, shaken. I'd seen him drink from the waitress at the waffle house. She'd had a look of utter bliss on her face. Me? I just felt pain. I couldn't hide the tremble that shook me from the inside out.

Ever so slowly, he withdrew his fangs, not missing my flinch. My hand jerked, but he held tight, not letting me pull away. I watched as he lifted his head, my blood staining his lips red. With a swipe of his tongue, he cleaned his mouth, then glanced down at my wrist, which was now a broken mess thanks to my self-inflicted wound and his puncture marks. Blood continued to ooze, and I felt my stomach churn. Pain was throbbing up my arm with each heartbeat. Again, I went to tug my arm away from him, but he wouldn't let go, and I feared he was about to slip into bloodlust and drain me dry.

"It's okay," he murmured, then scored his tongue on one of his fangs. A bead of blood appeared, and to my surprise, he ran his tongue over my wrist. The flesh began to knit back together immediately, and the pain vanished. He'd healed me. Then, and only then, did he release the hold he had on my arm. I sat back on my heels, not knowing what to think.

"Thank you." His voice was low, rough, and I didn't know what to say in response, so I shrugged.

"Have you had enough? You didn't take much." His face was no longer pale, and his cheeks had lost that awful hollow look.

"I could use more," he admitted, and my irritation returned. "For fuck's sake, just take it then. I'm not strong enough to drag you around. I need you to be on your own two feet." I offered my wrist again, angry that he'd stopped when he needed more.

"Thanks for dragging me this far." He sat up, ignoring my offered wrist, and ran his fingers through his hair, frowning at the mass of mud and twigs stuck to the back of his head. "Really? Feet first?"

"The feet are lighter." I shrugged, then watched as he vaulted to his feet and strode to the door, peering outside. When he stepped out into the rain, I clambered to my feet. "What are you doing? I'm not going to drag your sorry ass back inside if you collapse again."

"I'm rinsing off. I seem to have accumulated half a field of mud and twigs." Grabbing the hem of his shirt, he tugged it up and over his head, and I stood, hands-on-hips, unabashedly watching. Water streamed down his body, rivulets flowing across the dips and valleys before disappearing beneath the waistband of his pants. Turning his attention to the shirt, he rinsed it off in the rain before tossing it at me. I caught it, holding the wet bundle against my chest and basically enjoying the sight before me. I knew he knew I was watching, but I couldn't seem to turn away, couldn't close my eyes.

He was an Adonis. The water coursed over him; his palms ran over his chest to wash away any mud, then up, tilting his head back and running his fingers through the thick strands of his hair, eyes closed, neck exposed.

Blue lighting danced over my skin, setting up a

heat that warmed me from the inside out. I wanted him. I'd wanted him for a long, long time, but had kept myself in denial. But here, almost naked in the rain? I wanted him so badly that I feared I was about to self-combust. Tossing his shirt over my shoulder, I stepped out into the rain and moved toward him with no hesitation.

Lowering his arms, he watched me through hooded eyes. I kept coming at him, not slowing my pace, until I was flush against him, tugging his head down to mine. My mouth closed over his, giving him no escape, taking what I wanted because I wanted it oh so badly. He growled, and my toes curled in my shoes.

I refused to relinquish my claim on his mouth, couldn't have, even if I wanted to. He was just too delicious. His big hands roamed down my back, exploring every inch, and I shivered in delight, my tongue sweeping over him, brushing against a fang and not caring. Then I was being lifted until we were face to face, my legs clamped tightly around his waist, my fingers threaded through his hair. I was exactly where I needed to be and couldn't contain the purr that vibrated through me.

All around us, the rain fell, the wind whipped, and the thunder boomed, but neither of us noticed or even cared. I wouldn't have been surprised if steam was rising, given how hot I was for him. The kiss went on forever. My lips were swollen and tingling, and when he dragged his mouth away, I protested. I wanted more.

"Don't worry, I've got something better," he promised, his lips trailing kisses across my cheek and down my throat. There he bit, licked, and sucked, and I was squirming against him, my head thrown back. The rain splashing on my face only heightened my sensitivity.

"Bite me," I gasped, arching back further, so he was forced to place a palm between my shoulder blades to support me.

"You usually say that as an insult." He chuckled, licking the rain from my skin in delicious strokes of his tongue.

"Your last bite hurt," I reminded him. "Show me that it can feel good." Images of the waitress's face flashed through my mind. She had been in ecstasy from his bite. I wanted that, for despite his kisses being damn good, I knew there had to be more. All my life, I'd been craving more, needing more, demanding more from the lovers I'd taken to my bed, and none of them had been able to deliver. I was pretty sure Nate Wilder could.

He stilled at my words, frowning. "I hurt you?"

"In the warehouse. The first time we met," I reminded him. "You bit me then. To frighten me, I think."

"Didn't work." He shook his head, remembering. "And you're right. I need to make it up to you. Let me show you how good a vampire's bite can be." His mouth was back at my neck, sucking, pulling my artery up closer to the surface, preparing it with his tongue.

"Oh, I'm counting on it," I murmured, eyes closed, waiting with utter anticipation. I wasn't disappointed. The pop as his fangs pierced my skin didn't hurt, not even a twinge, and then his mouth sealed over the punctures, and he pulled my blood into his mouth, his growl telling me how good I tasted. But I couldn't think, only feel as sensations exploded. Fire and ice danced through my veins, traveling throughout my body until I was burning all over. My skin overheated, and stars exploded behind my closed lids.

When he lifted his mouth from my neck, I clasped his face in my hands and kissed him, tasting the coppery tang of my own blood, and instead of being repulsed...I was aroused. More aroused, if that was even possible. My hands squeezed in between us as I frantically kissed him, trying to undo his trousers but wrapped around him as I was, it was impossible.

He set me on my feet, hands steadying my shoulders when my legs threatened to buckle. The look on his face told me he wanted to undress me slowly, unwrap me like a Christmas present, but I couldn't wait—I had no patience for taking it slow. I'd waited too long, and I needed him now. The ache was painful. Pulling my tank up and over my head, I tossed it aside, then my bra, watching through hooded eyes as his hands went to his belt. We undressed, watching each other, the revelation of flesh almost my undoing.

"You are...stunning," he whispered, eyes traveling over my naked body. I stood proudly, letting him look his fill. He'd seen me naked before, once when I was unconscious and then after I'd flamed, but never in passion. This was different. We both knew it.

"So are you." Once I got over the magnificence of his chest and abs, my eyes trailed lower down to the corded muscles of his thighs. Damn, even his calves looked sexy.

Then the eye fuck was over, and we were in each other's arms again, hands traveling frantically, mouths open, seeking, finding, a collision of flesh and tongue and teeth. Curling a leg around the back of his knee, I toppled him, landing on top of him in the mud with a whoosh and a laugh. Then I was straddling him, my mouth on his in a frenzy I couldn't control—in fact, I was so out of control that afterward, when I examined it, it would terrify me.

With his hands on my hips, I slid down, impaling myself on the thick length of his cock, gasping as I stretched to accommodate him. I froze for a second, sitting upright, head thrown back, reveling in the sensations that were burning through me with each frantic beat of my heart. His hands reached up to cup my breasts, fingers teasing my nipples, and I opened my eyes to look at him. His gaze was on me, the gray of his eyes now glowing silver, his jaw tight. He was letting me set the pace, keep control, and it cost him everything he had. The feminine power made my lips curl, and slowly, I twisted my hips.

He sucked in a breath, his hands reflexively squeezing my breasts, hard. Pain combined with pleasure rocketed through me, and I moved again, swiveling my hips in a figure eight.

"Jesus," he ground out, biting his bottom lip, his control close to slipping.

I lowered my upper body to kiss him, sweeping his lip with my tongue, soothing the indent from his own teeth. He trembled beneath me, and the feeling of power was heady. With my mouth still on his, I raised and lowered my hips, sliding up and down the length of him, slowly. But I couldn't maintain the slow burn for long—by torturing him, I was torturing myself. My speed picked up, and his fingers dug into my hips, hard. He dragged his mouth from mine to my ear and groaned, "faaaarrrrkkkk." I almost came.

I wanted the release, wanted to orgasm so badly, and yet I wanted to prolong the journey at the same time. I'd never felt like this before. I'd had other lovers, but with Nate, it was different. It sounded clichéd, but the chemistry was off the charts, and I had a feeling we were only getting started.

Sitting up again, I resumed the twisting and rocking, trying to slow my own release, knowing instinctively that he would follow wherever I led. As if to confirm it, he murmured, "Whatever you want, Spitfire. I'm all yours."

His words did it. It was that simple, and that complicated. My body responded, and I shattered around him, my hips jerking as he surged up beneath me, thrusting, matching my movements.

My head was thrown back and the rain pouring over us slid over me, heightening every sensation, making our bodies slick as we rocked against each other. Over my own screams, I heard him grunt, knew he was with me, knew I'd met someone who could fulfill my every need.

I collapsed on his chest, panting, spent.

He chuckled as he wrapped his arms around me, holding me tight.

"Oh my god," I whispered, lost for words. How could I explain to him the sensations buffeting me, the wonder he'd just given me?

Chuckling, Nate wrapped his arms around me, holding me tight. "Do you have any idea how hot you are?" he whispered in my ear. "And not just because you're a fire demon!"

"Precisely. But now that you've gotten that out of your system, it's my turn." His words were pure sin, dripping in sex.

"What do you mean?" My breath hitched, and I tightened around him and felt his cock grow again, still inside me.

"It nearly killed me, Spitfire, letting you ride me like that." He was tracing patterns on my back with one finger, igniting a fire as he went.

I sat up, frowning at him. "You didn't like it?"

"I fucking loved it." His teeth flashed white in the night. "But we're only getting started. The first one was yours; the next is mine." Lifting me easily to my feet, Nate presented me with his muddy back. "Wash me off, would you, babe?"

My breath hitched. Babe. A term of endearment I'd never expected to hear, and yet, corny as it sounded, it warmed my heart. Obliging, I cupped my hands, capturing the rain, and rinsed the mud from his body. I may have lingered over his tight as-steel butt longer than was entirely necessary, and I flushed when he chuckled, but he stood still and let me have my way with him.

Once clean, he scooped me up and rushed us into the barn. I'd been expecting him to throw me down in the hay, but instead, he pushed me up against the wall, and I shuddered in delight.

"Do you trust me?" He growled; each word punctuated by gentle nips around my throat.

There was that word again, trust, the one we'd been throwing at each other since we met. This time I didn't hesitate, the word "yes" escaping my mouth before I had time to think.

"I want to taste you," he whispered, kissing me.

"You are. You have," I replied, our lips touching.

"Not everywhere," he murmured, voice low,

vibrating. "I want to taste all of you." His meaning was clear and had me clenching in anticipation and my mouth curling into a smile. Then his hands squeezed my breasts, and my head fell back against the wall with a groan. I cracked open my eyes and watched as he cupped them, holding them high, looking at them, then lowering his head, sucking first one nipple into his mouth, nipping with his teeth, soothing with his tongue, before turning the same attention to the other. So, this was what he meant by his turn...I was all for it.

I gasped, arching my back, sliding my thigh between his legs, rubbing his cock. With a growl, he dropped to his knees, and I grabbed his hair with both hands as he lifted one leg and draped it over his shoulder, his face level with my most intimate parts. I'd never seen anything so damn erotic in my life.

Then his tongue began stroking, sending shock waves through me. I felt like I was falling, my head spinning, and I wanted it to go on forever, but I also wanted to savor the moment. I was almost there, almost shattering, when he relented and lifted his head, only to replace his tongue with his fingers, softly stroking before plunging his fingers deep inside. I jerked back, my head hitting the wall with a crack. I was shaking, not sure I could hold myself up anymore.

"You're going to love this," he said against my thigh, kissing me there, keeping me on the edge with his fingers inside me but no longer moving, giving me a chance to catch my breath.

"Oh, I already am," I breathed, eyes closed, head back.

"Look at me," he demanded. I did, looking down at him with his face so close to the most intimate part of me. He smiled, revealing his fangs, and my breath hitched in my throat.

"You're not?" I gasped, suddenly unsure.

"I am. Trust me." I didn't stop him when he inched his mouth closer and closer to my throbbing clit. Then he sucked it, and I jerked again, bracing myself for pain.

"Relax." His fingers slowly started moving again, and I couldn't stop my hips from undulating, riding his hand, the response automatic. I wanted more. He delivered. His fang punctured my clit, and I screamed—not from pain—from the most intense orgasm of my life that threatened to send my head spinning clean off. It went on forever; it just wouldn't stop. I was vaguely aware of him standing, his hands clasping my hips as he pushed between my thighs and thrust into me, rough and hard, and I was screaming and screaming as wave after wave washed over me, around me, catapulting me into another universe.

"Good" was all I heard before his mouth was on mine, crushing me against the wall. I was on fire, unable to identify where his hands were touching me as the sensations I was experiencing threatened to overwhelm me.

When I finally came to my senses, we were lying on the straw by the fire, Nate curled along my back, his arms wrapped around me, my head tucked beneath his chin.

"What just happened?" I whispered, my throat hoarse.

Nate hugged me. "What do you think just happened?" he laughed. "You seemed to enjoy it."

I had a twinge of envy for every woman who'd ever been with him before me. It was as if I'd laid claim to him, now that I'd thrown caution to the wind—he was mine.

"Paige," he warned, sensing where my mind was going. "We both have pasts."

"You're right." I didn't want to tell him of my past lovers, and I sure as hell didn't want to hear about his.

"Get some rest." He kissed me, the softest, sweetest kiss, and I closed my eyes, sighing. I felt like I'd been traveling my entire life and had finally found home. With my body pleasantly aching and entirely satisfied, I did as he suggested, letting sleep claim me.

FOURTEEN

I woke to his kiss on my lips.

"Mmmmm." With a slow, languid stretch, I opened my eyes. Nate was lying on his side, propped up on one elbow, watching me.

"How are you feeling?"

"Good. You?" I wasn't sure how to act. Should I put as much space between us as possible since I'd just done the unthinkable and slept with a vampire? But I didn't want to move away. I wanted to be closer. I wanted more. Last night he'd satisfied my every need, but I'd awoken with a new hunger, a new need pulsed through me, and finally, finally, I'd found a man who could match me.

"We should get dressed, get moving." His voice

was low and deep, his eyes dark as they roamed over me.

"We could do that. Or..." I trailed my fingers down his chest and over those magnificent abs that I so admired.

"I like your idea better." Rolling me onto my back, he kissed me, long and hard, and I was arching beneath him, my legs wrapped around his waist, my fingers tugging at his hair when an amused laugh had us both freezing.

"Should have known." A female voice laced with amusement carried across the barn. Peering over Nate's shoulder, I saw a stunning woman standing there, with hands on hips, her black hair falling over her shoulder in a long braid.

"Raven?" Nate's voice held a tone of disbelief, and I shifted my attention to him. Did he know her? A twinge of jealousy had me stiffening beneath him. Not that he noticed. He was already untangling himself from my embrace, and just when I thought she was going to get an eyeful of his nakedness, she suddenly spun, presenting her back.

"Pants on, Wilder," she demanded. "I'll give you two a minute to get dressed." Then she was walking away, and I could hear her talking with someone outside.

Still flushed from our love play and body still thrumming with desire, I jerkily pulled on my clothes that had been laid out on the other side of the fire. Nate must have brought them in when I was sleeping.

"Who is she?"

"Raven Black. She used to work for the SIA, but now she's on the Council."

I wanted to ask more questions, but Nate was already striding outside. I carried my shoes closer to the doorway and sat to pull them on, watching the scene outside. Nate walked up to the black-haired beauty and wrapped her in a hug, then slapped the big man by her side on the back and shook his hand. They were friends, the three of them; that much was clear. The big man tugged Raven into his side and dropped a kiss on the top of her head, and my tension eased somewhat. They were together, a couple. Not that it mattered, I argued with myself. Nate was a free agent. He could do what he wanted with who he wanted. Liar, a voice inside my head screamed.

Smoothing down my hair as best I could, I stepped outside to join them, just in time to hear Nate ask, "What are you guys doing here, anyway? I was expecting an SIA rescue party, not a councilor and the Secret Service."

"When she heard your chopper had been shot down, there was no way I could stop her from coming and searching for you herself." The big man chuckled, then his eyes landed on me, and he stepped forward, offering his hand. "Alex Carter, ma'am, at your rescue. And this is my wife, Raven Carter."

"Raven Black." Raven corrected with an indulgent smile. "I kept my name. It's so unique." Raven gave my hand a squeeze.

"Paige Shelton," I responded automatically, a little overwhelmed by the powerful couple because they were *powerful*—I could feel it coming off them in waves. Add Nate to the mix, and it was mind-blowing.

"Sun's going to be up soon," Raven said to her husband. "We'd better get him out of here before he fries."

Alex winked. "If you insist." Then he was talking into his phone, and Raven turned her attention back to Nate. Their heads bent close together, voices hushed, so I couldn't hear. Affronted, I turned my back and headed toward the barn. I knew when I wasn't wanted, and those two didn't want me to know what they were talking about. Both of them glanced my way and then at each other, and anger started to niggle beneath my skin. They were talking about me.

"Don't mind those two. They've always been as thick as thieves." Alex Carter came and stood by my side, leaning back against the barn with his arms crossed over his chest.

"Have they been friends long?"

"A few years. Raven and I were working a case for the SIA that Nate was involved in—actually, he was a suspect." He laughed, remembering. "And the stubborn son of a bitch was determined to clear his own name without our help. Actually, I have him to thank for finally making me take action about my crush on Raven."

"Oh?" I didn't know why he felt this need to reveal all of this to me, but I was definitely keen to hear it.

"Yeah, Raven and I had been partners for years, and I'd liked her all that time, but she wasn't interested. Then Nate came along, planted a kiss or two on her, and I was suddenly anxious that I didn't have all the time to win her over as I thought I did. So, I made my move, and what do you know? Chemistry. Fireworks. And I won the girl." He chuckled at the memory. All I could focus on was that Nate had kissed Raven. He'd *kissed* her. I saw red and had to clench my fists to stop the fire from erupting from my fingertips.

"Carter!" Raven suddenly called, concern in her voice. "Whatever you're talking about, stop!"

Nate stepped towards us, but Raven caught his wrist, holding him back. My blood boiled at the sight of her touching him. What was wrong with me? Why was I so jealous? My mind was clouded, and I wanted to rip that black-haired bitch limb from limb.

"Jesus." Carter stepped away from me, looking at me in shock.

"What?" I grumbled, really getting annoyed now.

"Paige, take a breath." Nate shook Raven's hold off and covered the distance between us in rapid strides.

"What's everyone gawking at?" I snapped.

"You've got a little,"—Nate waved his hand, indicating my body—"Electric blue bubble going on."

Glancing down, I saw my entire body was shimmering with blue electricity. Great.

Nate raised his hand to touch my face, and

Raven called out to him not to touch me. My electricity spiked and turned to flame. I would burn her to the ground.

"Easy. It's okay." Nate kept his hand near my face, close but not touching. "Look at me. Just me. Don't worry about them."

I looked into his eyes, the stormy gray comforting, soothing. My flame sizzled, and as soon as it had left my skin, he slid his hand around to the nape of my neck, not breaking eye contact.

"Can you give us a minute?" Nate spoke to Carter, who nodded and quickly headed off to his wife, who was making noises about it not being safe for Nate to be near me.

"Ummm." Now that I was calming down, a wave of embarrassment took hold. This was not me. I was not a jealous person.

"Carter told you about how we all met, huh?" Nate kept his voice light and his grip on my nape firm. I nodded.

"Raven and I were never an item."

"Not that it's any of my business," I muttered, breaking eye contact and looking over his shoulder.

"If it bothers you, it's your business. And I'm kinda glad it bothers you." His admission brought my eyes back to his.

"What do you mean?"

"That I feel very possessive of you, Paige Shelton. I do not even want to entertain a single thought of any lovers preceding me. I imagine if I were in the position you are in today, I'd react...badly."

"You would?"

"I would." The words were whispered against my lips right before he kissed me, and the power of that kiss wiped out any thoughts of Raven from my mind. That kiss told me that right here, right now, Nate Wilder was all mine—if I wanted him.

We were wrapped in each other, lost in the kiss when Carter yelled at us to break it up. Nate lifted his head just as a big black Hummer busted through the trees and appeared in the clearing by the barn. I hadn't even heard it approaching; I'd been that wrapped up in Nate.

"Ride's here," Raven called, stating the obvious. I'd decided the best way for me to deal with my jealousy was to ignore her. So, I did. Nate wove his fingers through mine, and we approached the vehicle side by side. It was massive, its tinted windows designed to keep out the sunlight, I assumed; otherwise, Nate was going to have an uncomfortable ride back to Redmeadows.

"Hop in." Carter held the rear door open for us,

and I climbed up, grinning when Nate cupped my ass to help. "I think she's got it, man," Carter drawled.

"Just helping out a lady." Nate grinned, settling by my side and grabbing my hand again as if worried I'd scoot away. Carter and Raven rode up front with the driver, and I wondered if it was for my benefit—to keep us separated.

"They're riding up front so they can talk business without me overhearing," Nate explained, nodding at the partition that separated the front of the vehicle from the back. "Soundproof. Bulletproof. UV proof. Like I said, Raven is on the Council, Carter is with the Secret Service, and I'm SIA. Although we all work together on occasion, there are things they wouldn't want me to know, and vice versa. Plus, it's a security thing. If the vehicle were to be attacked, we wouldn't want all our high-powered people sitting in the one area, making it easy."

"You think we'll be attacked again? And who attacked our helicopter in the first place?" I hadn't given our crash too much thought until now. Still, someone had to have known the helicopter was traveling between Maxxan and Redmeadows and had been ready with whatever it was that fired at us.

"Carter is onto it. He doesn't think it's ghoul-related. Someone has been tracking SIA movements from Redmeadows. We think they had a tracker on the helicopter, and as soon as it was back in range, they fired."

"The danger never stops." It was an observation that wasn't wrong.

FIFTEEN

"Are you kidding me?" My mouth dropped open at the sight of my sister, Katie, dressed in the SIA black uniform, a red badge pinned on her belt. We'd arrived at SIA HQ, an impressive building entirely underground. Nate had explained the layout to me as we'd traveled down in the elevator. Level one was the Cadets and training facility, level two was for the Protectors, Nate explained the human equivalent would be Sergeant, level three was the executive offices— Nate's office, plus IT, payroll, and general admin, level four was the Enforcers—think Detectives, Level five was the Guardians—similar to Corporals, and the final level, all the way at the bottom was level six, the holding cells.

We'd gotten off at level four, where Nate explained he needed to brief the Enforcers on what he'd discovered in Maxxan.

Recognizing my voice, Katie's head swiveled in my direction, narrowed her eyes, and strode over. "What are you doing here?" She didn't sound pleased.

"Enforcer." There was a warning in Nate's voice.

"You're her boss?" To Nate. "You work here?" To Katie. Both ignored me. Katie rounded on Nate, her back ramrod straight, her jaw tense.

"You have no business bringing her here. You said you'd keep her out of it!" Fury underlined the accusation, and Nate frowned.

"She's safe."

"Oh sure, we know how easy it is to protect someone, so easy to keep them from harm." I'd never seen my sister so furious. Electricity danced over her clenched fists. "It was bad enough you dragged Rae into this, but now, Paige?"

"Calm. Down." His words were coated in steel, as cold as the look he threw at her. "You want to challenge me, Enforcer; you do it in my office, not here. Understood?"

My head swiveled from one to the other, wondering what the hell was going on.

"Understood." Spinning on her heel, she stalked away, only to suddenly turn and come back, her eyes on me. "You shouldn't be here. The SIA is not the place for you." I opened my mouth to protest, but she'd stalked away again. Nate's grip on my wrist stopped me from following.

"Give her some time. She'll calm down."

"What was that about?" I'd never seen Katie so angry nor so coldly determined. I'd seen her sad and in so much pain my heart hurt for her, but never like this.

"She'll tell you in her own time."

I tilted my head to consider him. His tense jaw and flashing eyes warned me not to push him on this. Not yet, anyway. And not here.

"Where's Rae?" I asked instead.

"Training. Out in the field. You might see her later. It all depends."

"On?"

"Developments here. And how she does in her training. She'll be gone for as long as it takes to get the job done."

"Are you talking...live training? As in real-life situations?"

"I can't discuss this with you, Paige. I'm sorry." Right. I wasn't SIA. Even though I was standing slap-bang in the middle of their headquarters, I was not a part of it. Even though it had been their helicopter I was riding in when it was shot down, I wasn't one of them. I didn't want to think my next thought...but it crept in, regardless. Even though I was sleeping with the boss. I sighed. It kinda hurt to be shut out, but I was smart enough to know it wasn't personal.

"Not until I appoint you an agent. If you want," he added.

My mouth dropped open. "You're saying I can join the SIA? But what about Katie? She won't like that."

"You've done some good work, Paige, even if your methods are somewhat unorthodox. You'd be better suited on this side of the law."

Realization dawned. "You were never going to arrest me." His grin told me I was right, and I punched him in the shoulder. Hard. "You could have told me," I grumbled. "I was picturing myself in a cell next to Uncle Frank."

"You had to learn to trust me first. And there is one thing I've learned from the Shelton women...you have to do things your own way."

"We are a stubborn lot," I agreed. "So, this,"—I waved my arm around, indicating the office space we currently stood in—"This was your plan all along? Recruit me into the SIA?"

"Not at all. I wanted you to stop hunting vampires before you got yourself killed. Then you proved yourself useful."

"And the rest?"

He knew what I meant, for he backed me up against a wall, crowded over me, and with his lips against my ear, whispered, "The rest is strictly off the record." And just like that, I wanted him. Lust washed over me in a tsunami of emotion, and I curled into him, pressing, seeking more.

"Patience." He chuckled, resting his hands on my shoulder and easing back. "We've got some work to do first, then I'm all yours."

Someone called his name, said they were ready for him. With a brush of his knuckles across my chin, he was gone, leaving me trembling. It took a solid minute to get my rampaging hormones under control. Then I followed Nate into the briefing room, silently sliding into a seat at the back of the room. Nate was addressing his agents, standing behind a podium at the front. I'd missed the beginning, but I quickly figured out they were discussing the ghouls, the missing girls, and Stillwater Pharmaceuticals.

Nate pointed to two agents. "McConnel and

Richards, I want everything you can find on Stillwater Pharmaceuticals—dig deep. Augustine and Darabi look into the ghoul angle. See if you can locate Leroy Byers. Shelton and Niles, you can run with the lead on this. You have twelve hours. I want a plan in place and patrols ready to go."

The room erupted into noise as Nate dismissed them.

"You missed something," I told him when he sat down next to me.

"Oh?"

"Who's looking into the helicopter crash?" It was playing on my mind. What if Nate was wrong? What if it had been the ghouls? What if their reach was wider spread and more powerful than we thought?

"The Secret Service has taken jurisdiction." His words comforted me somewhat. "Come on, you look dead on your feet. No wonder Katie was pissed at me."

"What time is it?" Now that he mentioned it, I was tired. Covering my yawn with my sleeve, I looked at him. We'd only gotten a couple of hours of sleep before Raven and Carter had found us.

"Ten a.m. Way past your bedtime."

Dawn had broken on the drive to Redmeadows,

but the tinted windows of the car had protected Nate, and the driver had dropped us off in the underground car park, negating the sun problem.

"Aren't you stuck here, though? You know, daylight?"

Threading his fingers with mine, he chuckled, pulling me to my feet. "Nope. The Secret Service aren't the only ones with fancy toys." And he was right. Riding the lift up to the parking lot, he led me to a silver Porsche Spyder, its windows so dark you couldn't see inside. At all.

"This is yours?" Running a hand over the car, I smiled. She was a beauty.

"Yeah. You like?" The remote beeped as he deactivated the alarm, then held the passenger door open for me to slide inside.

"It's gorgeous." Sinking into the plush leather seat, I closed my eyes and breathed in the smell. Leather and Nate.

"Play your cards right, and I might let you drive."

"Really?" I couldn't contain the excitement in my voice. Getting to drive a wickedly fast sports car was a dream of mine.

"One day."

He sped us through the streets of Redmeadows, up into the garden district. It was a beautiful and ornate neighborhood, with gorgeous historic houses and mansions, along with lush and green gardens. Nate told me the historic homes had been built by wealthy settlers, but now in this prestigious neighborhood, most houses had price tags that ran into the millions.

Nate's house was one of those. We stopped at the gates, and he used a remote attached to the visor to gain entry. The gates opened, and we drove up the long driveway, massive weeping willow trees flanking the drive. The house itself was a large Victorian, restored to its original grandeur, with white columns and the scrollwork of cast-iron balconies, definitely in the millions.

We pulled into the garage, the door sealing closed behind us, shutting out the sun.

"Welcome to my home." He was at my door, hand held out to assist me out of the car. I was slowly getting used to his vampire speed, but it still rattled me that one minute he was behind the steering wheel, and the next, he was standing at my door.

"Thank you." Placing my hand in his, I let him help me out. He was right about being tired. My eyes were gritty, and a headache was starting to niggle at my temples. He peered intently into my face. "What?" I grumbled, unnerved by the scrutiny.

"When did you last eat?" It sounded more of an accusation than a question. I shrugged, casting my mind back over the last few hours. We'd headed out to the Stillwater facility in Maxxan around eight. I'd had dinner beforehand, around six. Then we'd been busted, got shot down between Maxxan and Redmeadows, rescued, taken to HQ, and it was now...what? Ten thirty, eleven the following morning.

"Dinner last night."

"Fuck. And you fed me. Christ, woman, why didn't you say something?"

"Like what? We crashed in the middle of nowhere. Hey Nate, how about ducking out to get me a burger? I'm a little famished."

"Okay, okay, good point. But still. When we got to HQ, I should have gotten you something to eat."

"I didn't feel hungry," I protested. "I still don't." It was true. My stomach wasn't growling. I didn't feel like I needed fuel except for a headache that was probably an indication that starvation was imminent.

"Come on." Dragging me by the hand, he led me through the house to the most perfect kitchen I'd ever seen. You could fit my entire apartment in it. Opening the fridge, Nate frowned at the contents.

"What?" Peeking over his shoulder, I looked inside. "Oh." The problem was obvious. The fridge was neatly stacked with blood bags. No human food to be seen.

"Not to worry, I've had this problem before. I'll order in, you like Chinese? Pizza?"

Zeroing in on what he'd just said, I nailed him with a look. "You've had this problem before?"

"Yeah, when I first met Raven. She turned up here to question me."

"She came to question you, and you offered her food?" The snark was back.

Sighing, he shook his head. "I was helping her with her inquiries. She wanted to see the footage from my nightclub. I have a tech lab here. She was here longer than anticipated and got hungry. Nothing happened."

"You wanted something to happen," I accused, jealousy flaring again, crackling over my skin, the hairs on my arms standing on end.

"Babe." He began, but I cut him off.

"Don't call me babe!"

"All that ever happened between Raven and me is a kiss or two—and before you get all bent out of shape, I can assure you, kissing her—compared to kissing you—is like...like...kissing your sister!"

"Gross."

"Well, not gross entirely. But wrong. It felt wrong."

"Would you kiss her now if you got the opportunity?" I couldn't understand what was driving me down this path, why I felt so damn jealous and protective of him. So, we'd slept together, so he knew just how, where, and when to touch to elicit the most delicious response from me, so for once, I'd felt satisfied. So what?

"I don't want to kiss her. Two reasons. I've got you to kiss, and I like that much better. And two, Carter would kill me if I kissed her, and despite him being a wolf, I quite like the man. Not to mention those two are married with a kid. Not going to happen. Ever."

Dropping a kiss on my lips, he whispered, "I have every intention of allaying all your fears in that department very soon, but first, you need to eat. You're a little angry." With a grin, he straightened and pulled out his phone. I zoned out, not caring what he ordered.

Was he right? Was all of my weird behavior simply because I was hungry? Just then, my stomach growled, and I chuckled, placing my hand on it. Okay, okay, I was hungry; I admit it.

While we waited for my takeout, he took me on a tour of the house. All the windows had a UV glaze, keeping the harmful rays of the sun out. The house was breathtakingly beautiful and massive. I met his housekeeper, who came in during daylight hours to clean and deal with any callers who saw fit to visit during the day.

The lab in the basement was nothing like I'd imagined. We'd stopped before a thick steel-plated door, and he spoke his name into a box on the wall. The door clicked open, and I followed him inside. The underground bunker, for that's what it was, was massive and white. I'd been expecting cold concrete, maybe old brick, but what I saw took my breath away. It was divided into four rooms by glass walls. One contained banks of computers, servers, and other electronic equipment. Another held three medical gurneys, trolleys, refrigerators, and cupboards that I assumed stored medical supplies. The third room housed a large island bench with microscopes and other scientific equipment, and the last room held two big square cages. His personal holding cells, he told me. A hum buzzed through the air, and he explained it was the air filtration system.

We'd just finished the tour when the intercom buzzed with the announcement that my food had arrived, and this time I practically bolted up the stairs, my growling stomach dictating speed.

In the dining room sat a china dinner plate piled high with pizza. My smile was broad as I settled into my seat and grabbed a slice, shoving it into my mouth with little regard for good manners. At the end of the table was a black mug and Nate sat in front of it, bringing the cup to his mouth and taking a sip. Was that?

"I'm hungry too." Yep. Okay. It was blood. "Do you usually drink your blood from a cup?" I was curious. He'd drunk directly from the waitress's vein, as he had with me.

"I try not to drink from the vein unless I have to. There's plenty of bagged blood available. A few seconds in the microwave to take off the chill, and it does the job."

"Do you have a favorite type?"

"No."

I watched him take another mouthful, then turned my attention back to my pizza. It was delicious. I'd eaten three large slices before I slumped back, full.

"Good?" Nate had finished his beverage and was looking at me with a flush of color in his cheeks.

"It was delicious."

"Know what else is delicious?" The way he said it, the drawl in his voice, the hint of innuendo, had me grinning. "What?"

"This." Suddenly I was out of my chair, my butt lifted onto the table. He was wedged between my thighs and kissing me with a passion that stole my breath. When he finally allowed me a breath, I whispered, "That was corny."

"But true."

Within seconds we were naked, our clothes removed so fast I didn't feel them leave my body, just the delicious sensation of cool air against my overheated flesh. My eyelids fluttered shut as his hands glided over my shoulders, caressed my neck, dipped to my breasts, kneading. My eyes flickered open, and I watched the darker skin of his hands against the pale mounds of my breasts. Pleasure spiraled through me, hot and needy, and I ached.

One of Nate's hands glided down my stomach, toward where I wanted his touch the most. My hips moved forward, seeking.

"What do you want? Tell me. Ask for it," he

growled, bent over me, mouth at my neck, teeth scraping against my neck.

"Touch me, Nate. Please."

"Here?" He brushed his fingers ever so softly across my pussy, making me jerk. It wasn't enough. He knew it wouldn't be, bastard.

"Nate!" I demanded.

"Tell me." He moved his hand away as if in punishment. I had to tell him what I wanted if I was going to receive it. No more talking. I wanted to shout, make love to me.

"I want your fingers inside me." I panted. It was clear what he'd been waiting to hear, for suddenly I was whipped off the table and spun, so my palms were flat against the table, my feet hip-width apart, bracing. Waiting.

"You are magnificent," he said, his voice heavy. He traced a finger down my lower back, and a shiver danced through me. Some tiny part of my brain wondered at what point I'd lost my shirt? He kissed his way up my spine and grazed the back of my neck, smoothing my hair aside.

"The first time I saw you," he said, "I knew I had to make you mine. You were the sexiest, most stubborn, determined, fucking hot woman I'd ever laid eyes on."

"And I tried to kill you."

"I would have thought less of you if you hadn't." His words had the heady intoxication of a caress, and time lost all meaning. I licked my lips when I felt his hand slide between my thighs, caress my folds, then boldly slide inside, a long low groan of pleasure tearing from my throat.

"Is this what you want?"

"Is it too late to change my mind?" I breathed. He froze, his fingers inside me. I chuckled, "Your cock, Nate. Fuck me." While his fingers were magic and could take me higher, I wanted him on the journey with me.

I bit back the whimper as his fingers slid out, excruciatingly slow. Then his cock pressed against me.

"More."

He gave me an inch. I cursed the game he was playing but applauded it, too.

"More." Another inch. Still not enough.

"Is this what you want?"

"All of you. I want all of you."

He pounded all the way in, and I gasped; he groaned. But he didn't move, just left us both on the edge. I wanted to yell at him, rant at him to move, goddamn it, but I was incapable of speech. The ache was all-consuming, burning. Pulses of electricity sparked along my veins, demanding completion.

"You have all of me, Spitfire." He slid out and pounded forward, over and over, driving hard and deep. I climaxed, throbbing, screaming; the force of it raked over my nerve endings, leaving me raw and exposed.

"Paige," he roared, shuddering into me one final time, his hands digging into my hips, gripping, bruising deliciously. "Mine," he said, although I barely heard the word over the pounding of my heart.

SIXTEEN

We were in the briefing room on level four of SIA HQ, listening to the intel the SIA personnel had dug up on Stillwater Pharmaceuticals, when Katie silently sat next to me. I turned to look at her, but she was looking straight ahead, intent on what was being discussed.

"We propose two teams," one of the agents was telling Nate, "one to monitor the vans entering and leaving, and another team to follow where the vans are going when not at Stillwater."

"How many vans have you identified?"

"Five."

"I want a team on each van. They could be legit, and I don't want to waste all of our resources on finding out which ones are legit and which ones aren't. Six teams. One here, coordinating. The other five mobile. We stay on those vans until the shift is over."

"Sir? We don't have the numbers for six teams."

"Count me in," Nate responded, his eyes meeting mine over the heads of his agents.

"Fuck," Katie muttered under her breath.

"Why are you so against me being here?" I whispered. She wasn't as angry as yesterday, but she definitely wasn't happy.

"Not here. Come with me." I followed her to the elevator, where we rode down to the holding cells on level six. Well and truly out of Nate's earshot. We stepped out of the elevator and into the foyer area.

"Spit it out then." I waited, hands-on-hips, as she paced back and forth in front of me.

"This is a dangerous world, Paige," she began, clearly agitated. "It's not safe for you."

"Ummm. I guess Nate hasn't filled you in?" I shifted uncomfortably, wondering what she would say when she knew I'd been hunting vampires, on my own, in Maxxan.

"Filled me in on what?" She stopped and zeroed in with laser-like intensity, not blinking.

I decided the best way to do this was fast, like ripping off a band-aid.

"I've been hunting vampires. That's why Nate was in Maxxan. To investigate."

"First up, bullshit. Nate was in Maxxan to see if he could pick up the trail of the Gunslinger and Red Witch. Both of them are in the wind. We're tied up investigating the people going missing. Nate took it upon himself to do some fieldwork. Now explain. What do you mean, *hunting vampires*?"

My mind was whirling. Nate hadn't been there for me? I knew he'd said he'd never intended to arrest me, but I had sincerely thought he was there because he'd thought they had a rogue in Maxxan. To learn that wasn't the case at all was a shock. And to learn he'd been there searching for the Gunslinger when he'd told me he wasn't. He'd lied, and it hurt.

"Paige!" Katie snapped, drawing my attention back to her.

"Fine!" I snapped back. "I couldn't believe the SIA just up and left after they busted the Rampage drug ring. That they concluded we didn't have a vampire problem. So, I started hunting the vampires myself, since no one else was prepared to clean up the mess."

"Wait...how were you finding these vampires?"

"I'd dress—alluring—at a bar and hook 'em that way. Lure them back to an old warehouse I was using and kill them."

"Jesus, Paige! Were those vampires actually guilty of anything?"

"That's what Nate said." I pouted. I'd honestly thought I'd been doing the right thing, but it was becoming glaringly obvious I'd made a colossal mistake.

"Oh, Paige." Katie heaved a big sigh and ran her hands over her face. "You can't go vigilante. You just can't. There are consequences."

"So I'm learning."

"What has Nate decided?"

"Well, I'm not going to jail." I grinned sheepishly.

She shook her head. "That's something, at least. Don't tell me. He wants you to join the SIA too. If you're out there killing vamps on your own, you've got skills. And balls. Two requisites for the SIA."

"Anyway," I said, suddenly changing the subject, "what are you doing here? You never told us you worked for the SIA."

"That's because it's safer if you don't know. Then Jordan goes and ropes in Rae, and Nate has gotten you involved. Fuck it, Paige, I couldn't bear it if anything happened to you. I just couldn't." Tears welled in her eyes, and I wrapped my arms around her, hugging her tight.

"Nothing is going to happen to me. I've got kickass skills. And Nate will protect me."

"He won't always be there." She sniffed, squeezing me tight. We embraced in silence, each of us thinking of the past, of Katie's pain. She'd left town after the incident. We'd had no idea she'd joined the SIA, had only seen her recently when she'd returned for Grandma's funeral, and had left just as quickly as she'd arrived.

"I'm sorry about what happened." I sniffed, my own tears falling at what had happened to her. "But you can't protect me from every little thing. I'll do my best to stay safe, but that doesn't mean wrapping me in cotton wool."

"If I'd known what you were up to in Maxxan, I would've come down myself and locked you in the basement," she growled.

"Well, you didn't, and here I am."

Releasing me, she stepped back and smoothed her palms over her shirt before wiping the tears from her cheeks.

"There's probably something else I should tell you," I admitted.

"You don't have to. I can smell him on you, and if I got close enough, I'm sure I'd smell you on him."

"Rae says he's a good person?" I didn't mean it to be a question, but it came out that way.

"He is. He has history, but who doesn't? Since he's been the Director of the SIA, he's led a pretty upstanding life. Too busy to get into mischief." She winked, then grabbed my hand. "Come on, better get you back to him. Don't want him tearing my head off."

"So...you never bought into Dad's 'all vampires are evil' bullshit?" Was I the only one? The only one who didn't see the prejudice for what it was?

"I believed it, all right. Until I came here. We were very sheltered in Maxxan, Paige. We didn't even know what we were capable of as fire demons, let alone how many other species were out there besides vampires and werewolves. They are sooooo many. And they're not all out to get us. Is that a problem with you and Nate?"

"It was. At the start. When I tried to kill him." I shuffled my foot, feeling ashamed of my judgmental behavior.

"I would have liked to see that," Katie chuckled.

"You wouldn't. He kicked my ass."

"Sounds like you needed it."

"Thanks." I snorted, then snapped my mouth shut when the elevator dinged, and Nate stepped out, his eyes immediately zeroing in on me.

"Wondering where you got to." He looked from me to Katie and back again.

"Relax. Just having a sisterly chat," Katie told him, heading to the elevator before the door closed. "Let's do dinner soon, sis."

"Yeah, okay." I waved, relieved that we'd had the chance to talk.

Nate's face softened. "All good?" he asked.

"Yeah, all good." Grabbing his hand, I waited until the elevator had whisked Katie up, then pressed the button. "You know about Katie, right? What happened?"

"I know."

"That changed her. She just wants to keep me safe. Keep her family safe. I'm guessing she wasn't happy when Jordan showed up with Rae?"

"Nope, she wasn't. Let her displeasure be known too." Nate rubbed at his jaw in memory.

"She hit you?" I gasped.

"Punched more like it. Bloody hard too. That girl has a mean right hook. Reminds me of someone."

"I'm sorry." I apologized for my own behavior and Katie's.

"Why? Katie can fight her own battles, and she had a point. I should have given her the heads up that we were recruiting one of her family members."

"I'm surprised she didn't hit you again when I turned up."

"Probably didn't want a repeat of last time."

I digested his words for a moment. "What did you do?"

"She spent a day in the cells."

"Nate!"

"What? I can't allow my staff to think it's okay to go around punching me in the face." He had a point. I didn't get the chance to dwell on it anymore, for the elevator arrived, and Nate crowded me inside, backing me up against the wall and ravishing my mouth. I was flushed, and my lips were swollen when we arrived at the parking level mere moments later.

"What's the plan?" I had to clear my throat and start again, since my voice came out on a squeak.

"You're coming with me. We're team Delta, and we'll be assigned to follow one of the vans leaving the Stillwater offices."

"And Katie?"

"She's on team Bravo." He hadn't grounded her then because of me.

We were assigned an unmarked vehicle, and off we went into the night, Nate behind the wheel, me armed with night vision binoculars since I wouldn't be able to track diddly squat without them. I got the sneaking impression Nate was humoring me on this mission, letting me come along just to keep me out of trouble.

It kinda worked. We couldn't have been much past midnight when I fell asleep on the job, my head against the side window. We'd been given our assigned van to follow and had dutifully followed it back and forth, from a warehouse near the docks, back to the Stillwater building. I hadn't seen anything untoward.

Nate had radioed in the location of the warehouse at the dock and requested reconnaissance for the contents, but since we were all out playing follow the van, I wondered who was left to go and check the contents. Maybe that was tomorrow night's mission? Or the day shift? Which had gotten my brain to thinking—why was Stillwater Pharmaceuticals moving what I assumed to be a product at night? And that's when I'd finally succumbed to the exhaustion that still lingered from the night before.

I didn't wake until I was swung up into Nate's arms. "Shh, go back to sleep."

"Where are we?" I mumbled, tucking my head against his chest, eyes closed.

"Home." I liked the way it felt and loved the way he said it. As if I belonged here. Sliding into bed behind me, he wrapped his arms around me, and we slept.

IT WAS early afternoon when I woke. Nate was out cold next to me, and as quietly as I could, I slid out of bed and made my way to the bathroom. After using the facilities and having a quick shower, I dressed in the new clothes he'd had delivered especially for me and made my way downstairs, stomach once more growling. My body clock was all out of whack. I wasn't used to nocturnal living.

Opening the fridge to get myself something to eat, I laughed softly. Blood bags. Of course. I was considering my options when my phone dinged. A message from Katie inviting me to lunch. Perfect. After sending her a text accepting, she sent me directions to the Witches Brew Restaurant in the Bell District.

I scribbled out a note for Nate on a napkin and left it on the kitchen bench. No one was around when I let myself out the front door.

It took me half an hour to reach the Bell District. I was on foot since I didn't have a vehicle, but it was a gorgeous day, and I enjoyed the walk. A gentle breeze brushed my skin, and the sun didn't have the same intensity here, making outdoor activities much more bearable. My nose told me I was getting close by the delicious aromas in the air, plus the outcropping of art galleries, restaurants, and bars.

A smile pulled at my lips as I practically skipped along, happy, looking forward to spending more time with my sister. And then the trouble started.

I'd been walking along the streets, peering into shop windows, admiring a particularly stunning handbag in a boutique store, when a car screeched to a halt behind me. In the reflection of the window, I saw two men jump out and head toward me. I was mid-turn when one of them wrapped an arm around my waist and clamped a strange-smelling cloth over my nose. I sucked in a breath, trying to scream, but all I got was a lungful of the noxious fabric, and passed out.

I came to a little in the car. I was in the back seat, one of the thugs next to me, the other driving.

"She's waking up. Give her another dose. These bloody paranormals are fucking super resistant to everything."

"What's—" I was cut off mid-question by the cloth over my nose again and that funny smell. I caught a glimpse of buildings whizzing by outside the window before my eyes rolled back into my head, and I was out for the count.

SEVENTEEN

I woke up with a pounding headache and nausea that made my stomach churn. I was lying on a semi-hard surface, a cot of sorts, pushed against the wall of a white room. When I sat up, my head swam, and I cradled it between my hands while I waited for the world to right itself. Whatever they'd drugged me with made me feel like crap. There was a bench attached to the wall opposite, and sitting on the bench, a bottle of water. Groggily, I made my way to it and twisted the lid off, taking a long swig.

I surveyed my surroundings and immediately noticed my new attire – a scratchy, tissue-paper-like coverall. It was far from comfortable, but at least it spared me the embarrassment of being naked. As I glanced around, my gaze fixated on the massive glass wall that offered an uninterrupted view of what I could only assume was my cell. Across the hall, separated by a narrow passageway, I could see into another room. But it wasn't just any room; it resembled an examination chamber.

Inside, a chilling sight awaited me. A metal table dominated the space, its leather straps and buckles ominously dangling from its sides. Above, a movable overhead light, reminiscent of what surgeons use, cast a cold clinical glow. A trolley stood off to the side, further emphasizing the sterile atmosphere. Panic welled up inside me, an icy grip on my stomach. It was unmistakable—I was trapped within the walls of Stillwater Pharmaceuticals, and the foreboding thought that they intended to make me disappear loomed large. I couldn't simply sit here and let them carry out their sinister plans unopposed.

Eyeing the glass wall, I backed up, turned my shoulder, and ran at it full speed. My shoulder connected solidly with the window with an impact that rattled all the way through my brain, but I got nothing to show for it. The glass held, not even a crack.

Stay calm, I told myself. Nate would come. He

would find me. But until then, I had to be resourceful. After all, wasn't I the one who'd single-handedly killed thirteen vampires in Maxxan? I didn't want to remember that those vampires hadn't exactly been a threat. They'd been going about their daily business when I'd taken it upon myself to remove what I perceived to be a threat. I couldn't exactly complain when Stillwater Pharmaceuticals did the same thing.

A commotion outside my window caught my attention. Standing with my nose practically touching the glass, I watched as two men dressed in blue, guards I assumed, dragged a man wearing white coveralls like mine into the room opposite. In one smooth move, the guards had the struggling man down on the table, locking down his arms and legs in fast, sure motions. They'd done this before, were acting like a well-coordinated machine.

Then a stunning red-headed woman came into view. She wore a white lab coat and was talking to a short, balding man by her side. She glanced over at me, said something to the little man who looked my way, indicating something on the clipboard he carried. She nodded, looking satisfied, then stepped into the room where the man tied to the table was thrashing his head around and yelling. Although I couldn't hear a thing through the glass, it was apparent he was in great distress. A shudder ran through me, and I wanted to turn away, to not watch anymore, but I couldn't. I needed to see what they had planned.

The redhead stood at the foot of the table, watching dispassionately as the small man retrieved a syringe from his pocket. One of the guards held down the man's arm where it was jerking against its restraints, and the small man slid the needle into the vein and pressed the plunger. I caught a glimpse of green fluid. Was it the same green fluid we'd found in the vials in the Maxxan facility? Most of the samples had broken in Nate's pocket when we crashed, but the lab had been confident they could retrieve enough of the solution from the pocket itself, so Nate had left his pants with the medical lab. I wondered if the tests were back yet.

A minute passed. Then two. The redhead checked her watch, her face impatient. The small man was scribbling on his clipboard. Then the man on the table began to writhe and scream. I watched in horror as his face contorted and bones snapped and grew, his jaw elongated like that of a dog, his fingers curled into the table he was lying on, long wicked-looking claws appeared. The guards shuffled back a few steps.

"No..."

He was changing from human into something else. It looked like it hurt. A lot. And it seemed to go on forever as the man fought, thrashed, and struggled. But it was useless. Whatever they had injected into him was doing what they wanted it to do, for the redhead woman and the small man looked pleased.

Then the man on the table stopped moving. He was fully transformed. From here, he looked like a dog, but I wondered if perhaps he was a werewolf. The redhead looked at her watch, then nodded. The man was no longer a man, but a beast. His chest rose and fell in big puffs, his head flopped to the side, and I met his yellow eyes. His tongue flopped out from his snout and a trickle of blood dripped from his fangs. Fangs? Was he part vampire too? Most likely bit himself in the transformation. Another minute ticked by, and then it started all over again, the writhing, the screaming. This time, the bones were shrinking. The wolf's snout disappeared back into a human face, but the fangs remained wicked looking. His skin changed color, now gray, but the claws remained on the ends of his fingers. What were they doing to him?

Something must have gone wrong at that point, for suddenly, the red-headed woman was yelling. She was pointing at the man on the table and gesturing for the small man to do something. The small man dropped the clipboard and dragged the trolley over to the bed, shooing everyone away. An oxygen mask was slipped on the man's face and paddles to his chest. Shocking him back to life. Only he wouldn't come. Didn't want to come more likely.

Silent tears fell as I watched. It all fell into place. The humans who were disappearing, the homeless, and those who wouldn't be missed were being experimented on. They were turning them into beasts. Only from what I'd just witnessed, it wasn't going well. The red-headed woman slammed out of the room, anger in every step. The guards remained stoic, hands behind backs, eyeballs straight ahead, while the small man threw the defibrillator across the room. Their subject was dead. The previously pristine room was now splattered in blood and gore from where the man's bones tore through his flesh.

I turned my back, not wanting to see anymore. Soon, they would come for me. Soon, it would be my turn. I had to be ready. I had to escape.

Only they didn't come. No further experiments were undertaken, at least not in the room across from my cell. First, I got thirsty. Then I was hungry. I'd long since finished the bottle of water. I banged on the glass wall, trying to get someone's attention, but no one was there. Had something happened? Had they abandoned the facility, leaving me here to die?

But the air was still on. I could hear the slight hiss as it was fed through the ventilation tube attached to the ceiling. And the lights remained steady.

"I am not going to die here," I said out loud. The cell I was in had to be monitored—they were probably watching me, maybe making me weak, so I wouldn't give them any trouble. *I've got news for them, I'm always trouble.* I called forth a ball of flame and played with it, tossing it in the air between my hands. Yeah, assholes, watch this.

A full day passed. Then another. I couldn't tell day from night. It remained constant, but time was passing. I'd been confident that once Nate knew I was missing that he'd find me. Where was he? He wouldn't leave me here. He promised to keep me safe. And Katie? She'd be searching for me, tearing the city apart. She wouldn't rest until she'd found me. I could count on them. They would find me, I was sure of it.

By the end of the third day, I wasn't so sure, wasn't so confident. My lips were dry and cracking, my throat parched. Hunger had come and gone. Now I was just thirsty. If I'd known that bottle of water would be my last, I would have conserved it. A few sips a day to keep me alive. If I'd known.

I had way too much time to think. About my family. About Nate. My growing feelings for him. I mean, what more did I need to trust the man? I had glowing references from my own family members who worked with him in the SIA. And I'd seen for myself his kindness and the steel that ran through him. Kind but fair. Wasn't that what Rae had said? And finally, I let my mind fall into the memory of our passion, let it wash over me in comforting waves. The way my skin pulsed when he touched me, how my blood boiled in my veins whenever he was near. I wanted him constantly, and okay, I was probably already a little bit in love with him.

So where was he?

They came on the morning of the fourth day. I tried to summon a fireball, but I could barely stand. That's what they were counting on, I realized. Two guards stood outside my glass window, one holding a fire extinguisher. The other typed something into the band around his wrist, and my glass wall slid up into the ceiling.

I leaned against the back wall, watching them, calculating my chances of escape. Pretty slim, but a girl had to try. I waited until the first guard approached and grabbed my arm, pulling me forward. I staggered, dizzy, and he waited until I was grounded before pulling me toward the corridor. "This way."

I knew where they were taking me. To the room opposite. Not far at all, and I didn't have much time. As soon as we were clear of my cell, I broke free and ran. The guard hadn't been expecting it, didn't have a firm grip on me. If anything, he was merely guiding me where he wanted me to go. His mistake. I summoned a feeble fireball and tossed it over my shoulder at them. I didn't hear any screaming, so I figured I'd missed my mark, but no matter, I was almost to the end of the corridor. If I could just get around the corner, I could regroup and ready myself to attack.

Two sharp prongs hit my back, sinking into my flesh and then jolting me with electricity. I went down hard, my forehead hitting the floor with a sharp crack, my whole body seizing with the voltage traveling through me. I tried to funnel the power of the Taser and use it to my advantage. Still, I couldn't force my body to obey while it was seizing. Within seconds, my eyes were rolling back in my head, and a feeling of utter hopelessness smothered me.

EIGHTEEN

This time, when I woke, I was ready. Writhing and twisting on the table I was strapped to, I summoned my fire and tried to burn the shackles holding me. Only they were no longer the leather straps I'd seen earlier. They'd switched them to metal, and it heated beneath my flame, burning my flesh. With a shudder, I extinguished my flame, exhausted from using up my last reserves.

"You are quite spectacular." I twisted my head at the sound of a woman's voice. It was the redhead, and up close, she was even more beautiful. Her skin was ivory white, and her hair was cut into a stylish bob that accentuated her long neck. How could one so pretty be so evil? I watched as she moved to the foot of the table and looked at me as if cataloging my body parts, one by one.

"Who are you?" I croaked, my throat dry, my tongue swollen. I felt like I had a mouth full of cotton wool.

"Set her up on some fluids. Now we have her properly restrained, she is of no risk to us. We need her strong before the process." She instructed the small man, who nodded and bustled around at the trolley that was fully stocked once more. He came toward me with an IV bag connected to a long, thin tube with a needle on the end.

"Small prick," he muttered, wiping my arm with something cold, then sliding the needle into a vein.

"I'm sure you do," I snarled. He ignored me.

"He's heard them all before." The redhead told me, drawing my attention back to her. The saline solution traveled down the tube, and I felt it the moment it hit my system, the coolness. It was refreshing, and I wanted to gasp in relief. Instead, I kept my face neutral.

"I'll ask again. Who are you?"

"I'm Keri Ridgeway. And this is Doctor Byers." Both names niggled at me; I'd heard them before, I was sure.

"And I'm at Stillwater Pharmaceuticals, right?"

"Indeed. You and the SIA were getting a little too close for comfort. We were trying to detain your sister, but then you showed up and made it all too easy for us."

"My sister?" Why did they want Katie? How did they even know about Katie? And the SIA? My head was pounding. Even though I had the drip providing nutrients my body needed, I was nowhere near one hundred percent. A solid forty at best.

"Well, any fire demon would do." Ridgeway shrugged, then glanced at her watch. "Do you think she's strong enough?" she asked the doctor. He examined a panel of displays I hadn't noticed earlier, and it was then I realized I'd been hooked up to some sort of monitor. Jagged lines danced across the screen, up and then down, erratic.

"We can try. If she doesn't make it, we can get another."

"What?!" I croaked. Get another?

"We know all about you, Paige Shelton. We know about your father, your uncles, your sister and brother, your cousins. All part fire demon. It was convenient that Katie was here in Redmeadows, but she was a little elusive to trap. Next time, I'll send a team out to Maxxan, a quick snatch, and no one would be any the wiser."

"No!" My shout bounced off the walls, and the bitch laughed. I wanted to kill her, rip her throat out, and send my flame burning down her neck, toasting her from the inside out.

"Yes, good, good." The Doctor was practically clapping his hands in glee, but I kept my eyes on Ridgeway. This was her plan; she was responsible for all of this.

"Look at her eyes." Ridgeway was smiling. "The fire in them. So impressive. Okay, Leroy, commence."

I struggled and pulled at the metal cuffs chaining me to the table at my wrists and ankles. They bit into my already burned flesh, but I ignored the pain. I watched in horror when the doctor approached with the dreaded syringe and its green contents. He slid the needle into the tube running into my arm, and I held my breath as the green liquid flowed down the line of the drip and then into my vein.

It burned. My body convulsed, arching off the table, pushing my neck back until I could see the wall behind me. My jaw was locked shut, so no sound escaped, and then I felt the bone crack, and I screamed and screamed and screamed. Then the wave subsided, and I collapsed, panting, bathed in sweat. I waited for the next wave, the one where my bones would break and protrude through my skin while my body tried to turn into something else, something it wasn't designed to be. But unlike the others, I didn't transform. Instead, my nerves caught fire and burned, a low boil at first but growing worse with every breath. And as much as I'd vowed that I wasn't dying here, in this place, I knew that I was, with every second, dying a little bit more.

I faded in and out of consciousness. I'd wake up, my body boiling. Ridgeway was no longer in the room, but the doctor was. My head flopped to the side, and I saw the two guards standing outside. How long had I been like this? The torture I'd witnessed had only lasted minutes before the victim had died. It felt like it had been minutes already. Maybe hours. The torment on my nerves was like a blowtorch being applied without respite or mercy. I couldn't stop the tears streaming silently down my cheeks.

I thought of Nate, how he would be pissed when he found out what they'd done. And Katie. My heart broke for Katie. She may not recover from this. Thoughts were pushed out of my head when another wave hit. Oh God, it hurt.

I was staring up at the ceiling, concentrating on

staying alive, when something...changed. A shift in the pressure of the room. Then I felt it, weak at first, but then the whole room was shaking.

"What the hell? What are you doing?" The doctor looked at me in anger as he held onto the edge of my table while the room shook around us.

"Nothing." It wasn't me. The guards outside had dropped into a crouch as the building trembled, and a rumble, getting louder, reached our ears. The doctor crossed to the door. "What's going on?" he demanded, stepping out into the corridor. The door swung closed behind him, and I couldn't hear their reply.

A loud boom shook the building again. Dust and debris fell from the ceiling, and I screwed my eyes shut, then risked a peek to see what the hell was going on. I was hoping the cavalry had finally arrived. That would be nice right about now. A plume of dust and smoke rolled with speed down the corridor, hurtling towards the guards and doctor, who had all fallen to the floor with the last explosion—for that's what they were. Explosions. Initially far away, but now closer. Nate was blowing up the building to get to me.

Smoke completely obliterated the corridor from

my view. I could hear the guards coughing, imagined they were crawling away, trying to find fresh air to breathe. Then the smoke slithered under the door and quickly filled the room. I was trapped. Tied to a bed with smoke burning my lungs. I coughed and tried to call out, but I was too weak. My eyes were streaming, and my lungs felt like they were full of acid when I saw them, through the smoke, striding down the corridor like vengeful angels. Three bodies, dressed in black, gas masks over their faces. SIA.

"She's here!" My door burst open. Then my head was being lifted, and a mask slipped over my mouth and nose. Oxygen. Clean, sweet, oxygen. I sucked in a breath, then another, until eventually, the acid in my lungs settled back to the burn I was fast becoming used to.

"Paige?" I looked into the stormy gray eyes of the man I loved and grinned, though he couldn't see it beneath my mask.

"What kept you?" I croaked.

"Traffic was a bitch," he replied, turning his attention to the metal cuffs restraining me. In seconds, he'd ripped them away. He gently removed the drip from my arm, and I was scooped up into his arms. "Got her. Let's go."

"Is she okay?" The worried voice belonged to Katie, who was keeping pace by Nate's side.

"Fine," I tried to reassure her, but I wasn't fine. I was still dying. Whatever they'd injected into me was poison, and while I hadn't transformed into some contorted beast, I was dying just the same. She was going to be so mad.

More explosions echoed behind us, and Nate picked up the pace. They were going to demolish the entire building, I realized. Not just rescue me, but end the evil experiments that were taking place here. I sighed a ragged, rattling sigh.

"Don't you fucking dare," Nate growled, squeezing me tight. "You hold on. You do not die today, you hear me?"

"If you say so." My throat was coated with razor blades and my voice as rough as rusty nails. This sucked balls. I'd never given much thought to dying before, but now that I was facing my mortality, I had one strong opinion. I wanted to die in my sleep. This fucking hurt.

I must have blacked out because the next time I opened my eyes, I was in a black room. All of it. Black. Walls, ceiling, floor. Either that or I'd gone blind.

"Easy." Nate had hold of my hand. "You're safe. We're at the SIA. You're in a fireproof room."

"I'm dying." I hated to state the obvious, but he needed to be prepared, needed to know there was no saving me. This was the end.

"Don't give up. Not now." The anguish in his voice tore at my heart. If only he'd come a day earlier. One day. Before they'd injected me with the green shit. It took too much effort to reply, so I squeezed his hand, only it wasn't so much a squeeze as a twitch. I was weak. Breathing was an effort. Keeping my eyes open was an effort, and it would be so, so easy to close them and stop fighting. Just let death take me away, end the pain.

"Flame. I need you to flame, Paige." The words were spoken by my ear. I felt the puff of his breath, yet I barely heard them. I just wanted to sleep and felt myself slip a little further away.

"NO!" Nate's shout jerked me awake. "No, goddammit, flame! Fight it, damn you. I know it hurts. I know you're tired, but you can't leave me, Spitfire."

I opened my mouth to tell him it was all right. It would be okay. I'd die, and he would move on with his life. But I needed him to take care of Katie. My mouth moved, and I tried to tell him, but the words wouldn't come. Seeing my struggle, he cupped my face, his eyes swimming with tears, and the sight was so unexpected I blinked in surprise.

"I love you," he whispered. "I should have told you sooner. Fuck. I thought we had time. Paige, please don't leave me."

Words I had never thought I'd hear from his lips. Powerful words. Words I wanted to hear again. Through my clouded mind, I tried to remember what he had asked me to do.

"Flame, Paige. Flame." He let me go and stepped back. Right. I needed to heal myself with my flame, be consumed by fire. Only it was going to be difficult since I was already incredibly weak. Did I have the strength to call forth my flame? I had to try. I had to try for him and Katie.

Closing my eyes, I concentrated, centering myself. I felt a warmth on my hand, heard him encouraging me.

"Yes, that's it. Just a little more, and you've got it." But then the shimmer of flame on my hand went out; I lost it. Try again. While the short burst of flame had drained me, it also empowered me. Yin and yang. It was my last shot at survival, and if I wanted to hear those words again, I couldn't blow it.

Digging deep, I gave it everything I had, pulling

from my very core, gasping with my last breath. It hurt. Almost as much as the green liquid when it first hit my veins. This was my dying flame. It erupted over me in a whoosh, and I faintly heard Nate say, "Jesus!" Then I was floating, flames dancing around me, inside and out, up, up, and away. The pain was gone, in its place, euphoria. It was heady and addictive, and I didn't want it to end, feared it would stop all too soon and I'd either be healed or dead, for I had used my very last essence to draw the flame.

I drifted in and out of consciousness now, all the while burning. I caught a glimpse of the black room, and then I slid away again. I heard voices but couldn't make out what they were saying. I heard begging and pleading, not in words, but the emotion. So much emotion. It called to me, pulled me close, almost to the edge, but then the flame pulled me back into its welcoming embrace, and I succumbed to the fire once more.

Minutes turned into hours, hours into days, days into years, years into decades...then eternity. That was how long I burned. The earth kept turning, and I kept burning. Then, all too soon, it was over.

"Welcome back." The ragged relief in Nate's

voice jolted me awake. He was sitting on a chair by my bedside; my hand clutched in both of his.

"Hey." I tried to give him a reassuring smile but suspected I didn't quite pull it off by the frown pulling his brows together.

"I thought I'd lost you."

"As if it were that easy," I mocked. "I'm a vampire slayer."

Before he could reply, the door burst open, ricocheting off the wall. Katie was by my side, hands on hips, fury radiating out from her. "Don't you EVER do that again!" Then she burst into tears, the anger gone.

"Come here," I whispered, holding out my arms to her, and she collapsed onto me, her wet face buried in my neck. Wrapping my arms around her, I cried, too. We weren't big criers, the Shelton's, but when the occasion called for it, we did it with gusto, great big snotty sobs. Nate left, only to return with a box of tissues.

Eventually, the emotional storm passed, and Katie pulled away.

"It was you they were after," I told her, mopping myself up with a tissue.

"What?" Nate and Katie said in unison.

"They know about Katie—about all of us

Shelton's being fire demons. They were trying to capture Katie, but then I turned up an easier target."

As if he couldn't stand to be apart from me, Nate picked me up, settled himself on the bed, then nestled me between his legs, my back against his chest, his arms curled around me. I didn't protest.

Pulling up the chair, Katie sat down. "What else can you tell us?" she demanded.

I told her what I knew, what I'd seen on the first day—the woman, Keri Ridgeway—but paused when Nate sucked in a breath.

"She used to be the director of the SIA. Should have known. She disappeared when we discovered she'd been kidnapping humans and experimenting on them, trying to turn them into some super paranormal hybrid. She failed."

"Well, she's still at it."

"I find it interesting that she hasn't changed her name or appearance. That's a whole other level of cockiness. She knew the SIA wanted her, and yet she set up shop—again—right under our noses."

"Well, we've shut her down this time." Katie crossed her arms and leaned back. "That building is nothing but rubble. Fed the humans the faulty gas line story."

"Did you get her? Ridgeway? Was she in the building?" I asked. I saw the look Katie gave Nate.

"She wasn't, was she? Or you can't account for her. Which means this isn't over. And what of the doctor... God, what did she say his name was?" I rubbed at my forehead, trying to remember. "I've heard it before. I don't know why I can't remember it!"

"Because you've always been shit with names," Katie interjected.

"Where do you think you've heard it?" Nate prompted. Bless him for trying to help me remember. "Here?"

"No. A while ago. In Maxxan...was it one of the interrogations?" I said, more to myself than anyone else.

Nate stiffened behind me. "It wasn't Leroy Byers, was it?"

"Yes!" I exclaimed. "That's it." Then I remembered where I'd heard it. The ghoul we had interrogated, Ian Blackwell, had told us that Leroy Byers was a powerful ghoul, and we'd find him hanging out at a nightclub. The small balding man I'd seen would stand out like dog balls at a nightclub. Ian had only given us half the truth.

I described Leroy's appearance, how Ian had tried to throw us off track.

"Clever," Nate muttered, "but now we know what he looks like. Unless he changes skins."

"Urgh." My stomach heaved at the thought. "If Ridgeway has started up once, she can do it again, and with Byers able to change appearance at the drop of a hat, how can we possibly stop them? There is still the Stillwater facility in Maxxan. Didn't you say that's where they make the drugs, Nate? So that green shit they injected me with, it's made there. They still have a supply."

"She's right," Nate admitted to Katie.

"Right. We need a team in Maxxan. Immediately. And I want a protective detail on my family. All of them," Katie barked, taking charge. I couldn't contain the pride I had for her.

"We're going to have to pull in extra resources," Nate replied. "Take the lead, will you, Katie? Jordan and Rae will be redeployed back to Maxxan early. Rae will have to train on the job. As will you." Nate squeezed me.

"I'm still in? Even though I got myself captured?" It had been humiliatingly easy to kidnap me.

Katie made a snorting noise. "You were in the minute he laid eyes on you."

"No." I didn't believe her. Nate had beaten the ever-living shit out of me when we first met.

"Pft. I'm rarely wrong. Ask him. But,"—she held up a warning hand—"on your own time. We've got a psychopath to take down."

"Actually, I think you have four."

"Explain," Katie demanded.

"I saw the Gunslinger and the Red Witch while I was being held in their lab. I was mostly out of it, but I swear I saw them both. They were in deep discussion with Ridgeway. I think they're in this together."

"This changes everything." Nate's voice was stone cold, and he set me away from him. "We already have an AOD out on the Gunslinger."

"AOD?"

"Apprehend or destroy," Katie filled in.

"And the Red Witch?"

"AO," Nate responded. "Apprehend only. But I'm upgrading it to AOD. Same with Ridgeway and Byers, although it will be tricky to prove his identity. Katie, get the paperwork ready, and I'll authorize it. Organize a team to head out to Maxxan ASAP. We'll set up headquarters at your grandma's old house. Rae has already given approval, and I checked it out when I was there. It will suit our needs perfectly. I want that cave beneath the house converted into cells. The rest do as you see fit. Swing by my office, and I'll authorize finance. Get whatever you need."

Katie hurried to do his bidding, and I watched, sitting cross-legged on the bed as Nate paced back and forth, lost in thought.

"When are we going home?" I eventually asked, wanting nothing more than a hot shower and a change of clothes.

"To Maxxan? We're not. I'm not risking you. Not again. We stay here, in Redmeadows. I'll build you a closet as big as your apartment, filled with every designer label you can ever imagine if it will persuade you to stay."

I smiled, slid off the bed, and padded toward him, clad in nothing but a very unattractive hospital-style gown that I suspected gaped open at the back, judging by the breeze I felt on my naked ass. Sliding my arms around his neck, I pulled his head down and kissed him.

"I'm going to take you up on the closet, Wilder," I whispered, "but when I said home, I meant your place. You're my home."

"When you say shit like that..." he ground out, his hands clenching on my hips so hard I knew I'd have bruises—and I didn't care.

"Mmmmm?" I purred. "When I say shit like that...what?"

"How did I get so lucky to have you stumble into my life?" He chuckled, low and rumbling.

"Stumble? Hardly." My smirk was full of confidence. "I caught you, fair and square."

He laughed. "Caught me? That's not how I remember it. We had a deal; winner takes all, remember? And I won."

"So, take me," I taunted, tilting my head back, arching my hips against him.

His mouth came down on mine, and no more words were needed. The two of us? We were one. He had my heart, all of it, not the tiny little piece that I'd thought he'd stolen from me, but the entire bloody thing. And I couldn't be happier. Tomorrow, we had a vampire, witch, and ghoul to hunt. But tonight? Tonight, he was all mine, and I didn't intend to share.

Next up in the Enforcer series: Join Katie & Brax in **Capture the Night** for another heart-pounding adventure.

www.JaneHinchey.com/Enforcers

Thank you for reading! If you enjoyed this book, I'd greatly appreciate your review.

You can find a complete list of my books, including series and reading order on my website at:

www.JaneHinchey.com

Join my newsletter here:

www.JaneHinchey.com/subscribe

And finally, join my readers group on Facebook here:

www.JaneHinchey.com/LittleDevils

Thank you so much for taking a chance and reading my book . It's readers like you who make this journey worthwhile and fuel my passion for storytelling. Your support means the world to me, and I can't wait to share more exciting stories with you in the future.

xoxo

Jane

FREE BOOK OFFER

Want to get an email alert when a new book is released?

Sign up for my newsletter today,

https://janehinchey.com/subscribe

and as a bonus, receive a FREE e-book of **Cupcakes & Curses!**

READ MORE BY JANE

Find them all at www.JaneHinchey.com/books

<u>The Ghost Detective Mysteries</u>

#1 Ghost Mortem

#2 Give up the Ghost

#3 The Ghost is Clear

#4 A Ghost of a Chance

#5 Here Ghost Nothing

#6 Who Ghost There?

#7 Wild Ghost Chase

#8 Easy Come, Easy Ghost

#9 Life Ghost On

<u>Witch Way Paranormal Cozy Mystery Series</u>

#1 Witch Way to Magic & Mayhem

#2 Witch Way to Romance & Ruin

#3 Witch Way Down Under

#4 Witch Way to Beauty & the Beach

#5 Witch Way to Death & Destruction

#6 Witch Way to Secrets & Sorcery

The Gravestone Mysteries

#1 Fur the Hex of it

#2 Battle of the Hexes

#3 What the Hex

The Midnight Chronicles

#1 One Minute to Midnight

#2 Two Minutes Past Midnight

#3 Third Strike of Midnight

Clean Scene Inc.

#1 All in Vein

PARANORMAL ROMANCE/URBAN FANTASY

The Awakening Trilogy

Hell's Angel Trilogy

The Enforcer Series (4 books)

Standalones

Returned

Secret Fates

Destiny's Touch

Blood Cursed

Heart of Darkness

ABOUT JANE

Hi there! I'm Jane, crafting tales of paranormal cozy mysteries sprinkled with urban fantasy romance. Between sips of coffee and dodging my mischievous cats, I immerse myself in stories where magic meets everyday life.

Once known as Zahra Stone in the world of steamy urban fantasy, I've now merged those fiery tales under the Jane Hinchey banner. Off the page you'll find me binging on true crime documentaries or sneaking in a power nap. Dive into my stories and join me on an enchanting journey!

Find me here: www.janehinchey.com

facebook.com/janehincheyauthor

instagram.com/janehincheyauthor

amazon.com/Jane-Hinchey/e/B0193449MI

bookbub.com/authors/jane-hinchey

goodreads.com/jane_hinchey

www.ingramcontent.com/pod-product-compliance
Lightning Source LLC
Chambersburg PA
CBHW051245210726

48287CB00002B/362